Clin   ixon
for   aped
and   worst
of t   as of
the   the
vici   es he
bec   hired
out   n, at
last   and
mac   n hot
red

JORNADO

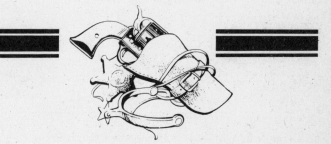

E. R. Slade

ATLANTIC LARGE PRINT
Chivers Press, Bath, England.
John Curley & Associates Inc.,
South Yarmouth, Mass., USA.

Library of Congress Cataloging in Publication Data

Slade, E. R.
  Jornado.

  (Atlantic large print)
  Reprint. Originally published: New York: Manor Books, 1979.
  1. Large type books.   I. Title.
  [PS3569.L22J6 1985]   813'.54   84-28491
  ISBN 0-89340-849-2

British Library Cataloguing in Publication Data

Slade, E. R.
  Jornado.—Large print ed.—(Atlantic large print)
  I. Title
  813'.54[F]   PS3569.L22

  ISBN 0–7451–9099–5

This Large Print edition is published by Chivers Press, England, and
John Curley & Associates, Inc, U.S.A. 1986

Published by arrangement with Singer Communications, Inc

U.K. Hardback ISBN 0 7451 9099 5
U.S.A. Softback ISBN 0 89340 849 2

JORNADO

CHAPTER ONE

Under the star-speckled sky, Dead Flats, ghost town, was just broken shapes. There was not a sound but what the wind made. The place was emptier than any piece of desert, except for the Presence.

The Presence stalked the empty street, peered from the window and door openings making them seem blacker than eye holes in a skull, rustled with the wind in loose shingles, thumped with unseen loose shutters, and surrounded the lone rider like a fog.

Clint Evans rode slowly, carefully, his eyes watchful of the night. His concern was not with the Presence, but with the possible threat of singing lead. Clint never rode into a meeting like this without plenty of care. Twice in the past he'd nearly lost his life in crossfire.

In the blackness of a saloon's door opening, there was the slightest movement. Clint swung the barrel of his Winchester that way and drifted his mount into the deeper shadows of an alley just short of the saloon. He swung down with a creak of saddle leather.

The back door squeaked as he opened it on blackness. He'd seen nothing as he circled to

1

the rear of the saloon. Now, pistol cocked and tipped up in his hand, he stepped inside.

There was a scurrying in the dark. A board creaked.

Clint moved forward. There was the faint smell of whiskey and sweat for a moment, then the air currents changed and the smell was gone.

Clint sensed the bulk of the bar to his left and moved catlike behind it, noiseless as a shadow, and dropped down to rest his pistol hand over the mahogany.

For some moments he did exactly nothing.

A breath was drawn, with a slight wheeze in it, somewhere in the dark ahead of him.

'Señor Evans?'

'You alone?'

'Sí, Señor. I am alone.'

'Strike a light.'

'Of course, Señor. But do not shoot, eh?'

In the flare of the match, Clint saw a narrow swarthy face with heavy brows and a worried expression. He also saw the crossed shoulder cartridge belts, and the rifle and the brace of pistols.

The match went out, and the large moving shadows that had surrounded them apparition-like engulfed them in total blackness once again. The wind moaned a little under the eaves, scraped blow sand in

2

grasses growing in the dark street beyond the doorway behind the Mexican—Clint heard this, did not see it. A shutter banged lightly away off somewhere, and something scurried in a corner.

'Talk,' Clint said. 'I don't like wasting time.'

'You are Señor Evans?'

Clint drew his knife from his belt and drove its point into the mahogany, then he struck a match and held it cupped in his hand so it lit the initials carved in the handle. Then he blew out the match and returned the knife to his belt.

'Let us find a lantern,' the Mexican said.

'No. What's your business?'

'It would be much better with a lantern.'

'No.'

The Mexican sighed. 'Perhaps you are right,' he said. He coughed. It was loud and wracking, startling in the eerie darkness. The Mexican sounded sick. Perhaps he had consumption.

'I come from Señor Griego. Señor Griego wishes to hire you.'

'Who the devil is Señor Griego?'

The Mexican's breath caught slightly in surprise. 'El Señor Griego? You have not heard of him? Señor Griego he is the big cattle man. He have a big hacienda. Very beautiful.

3

He had also the mines.'

'And what does he want of me?'

'It is the daughter. She is kidnapped. Do you know of the bandido Garcia Valenzuela?'

'I've heard of him.'

'He had kidnapped Señorita Pepita Griego.'

'I don't know much of Mexico.'

'You will not have to, Señor. The bandido Valenzuela he is in the mountains to the north. He had una plaza fuerte there. Una fortificación.'

'Tell the Señor Griego I am not interested.'

The Mexican did not speak for a moment, and he coughed.

A match flared. There was the Mexican, holding up a large handful of double eagles.

'It is all American money,' he said, and held it out.

The match went out. Clint had not moved.

'Go back to Mexico,' Clint said. 'I'm not interested.'

Clint heard his horse stir outside. He was abruptly very alert, knowing his horse well.

He had already slipped halfway to the rear door when from the gaping opening on the street there came a flash and roar. The Mexican screamed and it was cut short by a second shot.

It was not Clint's fight. He was by this time out the rear door and moving swiftly through

4

the dark to the place where he'd left his horse.

White Socks was not there.

Clint stood still a moment, listening.

He heard scuffing hooves somewhere along the main street, the careful step of someone inside the saloon.

Clint glided on down the alley and peered into the street, pistol ready in hand. He could make out the vague shapes of horses being led away south down the street. Clint, who had quit smoking some years earlier because it had made him a target one night and nearly cost him his life, had taken the habit of chewing a toothpick. Unconscious of his own action now, he stuck one in the left corner of his mouth and his lips moved so the end pointed up. He was thinking.

There was a scuffing in the alley behind him, and he pivoted, drawing, firing into the other man's muzzle flash. There was a sound as of a sack of potatoes being dropped onto the ground, the chink of metal against stone.

Clint chewed his toothpick a few seconds, then went cautiously to investigate. He took a chance and struck a match. Another Mexican, this one heavyset. Wearing a gaudied up gunbelt and wide sombrero. The nickeled pistol lay beyond the outstretched hand of the dead man. Clint checked the pockets, found one thing that interested him—a letter,

5

written in Spanish. He pocketed it without taking time to read it as the match went out. Then he moved quickly back to the end of the alley on the main street.

The horses were dissolved in darkness, but listening carefully he could hear the snorting of an animal—White Socks, he was quite sure.

He moved with great care along the street keeping to the deepest of the shadows, listening to the wind, the idle slapping of the shutter, the blow sand rattling in the weeds.

There was only one man with the four horses. He smelled strongly of sweat and tequila. As far as Clint could tell, the Mexican was peering off nervously down the street. Perhaps he was thinking of going to help his compadre.

Clint tried to slip up on the man from behind, but one of the Mexicans' horses moved just then and the head under the sombrero turned.

The Mexican started to go for his gun.

'Sóltela!'

The Mexican dropped his gun with a clatter to the ground.

'Manos Arriba!' Clint added, and could just make out the Mexican's arms lifting above his head slowly.

Continuing in Spanish, Clint asked him, 'Who are you?'

'I am just a poor sheepherder,' the Mexican whined, also in Spanish.

'Don't lie to me.'

'I am not lying. I tell you the God's honest truth.'

'Would you like a bullet between your eyes?'

'Please, Señor, no. Have compassion on a poor sheepherder.'

'Where are your sheep?'

'They are in the care of my young son, on a hillside not far from here.'

'What are you doing with my horse?'

'One of these is your horse, Señor?' the Mexican asked with exaggerated surprise.

'Go see to your dead friend.'

'Pedro is dead? Poor Pedro. He is always so hotheaded. He attempted to shoot you, no doubt. He is always doing foolish things. I am sorry you had to kill him, but that is how the world passes, is it not?'

'Get moving. Your gun will be where you left it when you get back. But do not try to kill me. You may have to follow your friend to hell.'

Clint rode away into the desert, going north. His jaw was clamped shut hard, the toothpick jutting like a spike from a cactus. He was not pleased at all. He did not like killing, particularly when he didn't know the

7

cause for it. But the thing was none of his business. He was clear, and glad of it. He had not trusted the messenger from Griego. He didn't like how any part of the thing smelled. He was not interested in getting mixed up in a Mexican feud. It was foolish for outsiders to take sides in those kinds of things.

He made camp perhaps two miles from town, in an arroyo not far from La Escalera Wells, named undoubtedly for the natural staircase formation leading down into a small canyon to the cistern-like hollows in the rock holding water. One never made camp right at a watering hole, since there were few places in this country more watched by Indians and other would-be ambushers. It was only a couple of years ago that he learned that the hard way.

For a few minutes he lay in his bedroll listening to the wind which ceaselessly wore at the landscape, and then he slept.

*   *   *

In the early morning, as the sun was just lifting above the eastern horizon, a flat hot red disk getting ready to scorch the desert once again, Clint chewed on jerky, watered White Socks from his hat and made ready to travel on northwest.

He mounted and looked around the horizon out of habit, saw nothing he didn't like and was about to set his mount going when he thought of the letter he'd taken from the man he'd killed. Curious, he got it out and read it over.

'Be jiggered,' he said aloud, glaring out over the cactus.

He swung his horse and rode south again, grim as a man bent on a lynching.

CHAPTER TWO

Through his mind went a scene he'd relived many times in the past five years. But the years had not blurred the image or dulled the sounds of the shots. If anything, the scene had become more vivid. He'd been riding home from rounding up some strays off on the southern range of his Colorado ranch, and had just topped a rise from which he could see the ranch buildings. He had always enjoyed this view, liking the way the neat set of buildings nestled against the dramatic backdrop of the big wall of mountains. Small clumps of cattle drifted the range between the rise and the buildings, grazing in the late sun.

But then the door of the house opened, and

he could just make out Margaret struggling with a man, and could just catch the sound of her screams, thin and desperate, over the wind.

He rode hell-for-leather, but was only about a third the way there before smoke began to rise from the ranch house and the horseman rode off with Margaret. He fired warning shots in the air, hoping to show he meant business, but the kidnapper ignored him.

He tried to cut them off, but they swung north into the mountains and it got dark before he could get near them. The next morning he went on following the trail and at noon came across Margaret's body, battered and naked.

After that he hadn't any stomach for ranching and began drifting keeping at eye peeled for the man who'd done it. To pay his expenses, he became a manhunter and sometimes hired out as a gun on gold shipments. In the five years since it had happened, he'd learned only one thing about the man he was after: he was called Blake Dixon.

The letter in Spanish taken from the man who'd gotten himself dead trying to kill Clint was addressed to Garcia Valenzuela. Translated it said, 'Many fine men have been ruined by greed. I assure you that I will settle for nothing less than what is due me.' It was signed, 'Blake Dixon.'

★   ★   ★

By daylight, the ghost town looked very different. The Presence wasn't gone, just hidden away in the dark corners and crevices like all other spirits of the night. The town was just a dried out old broken down bunch of buildings, a monument to greed, haste, and decay. The wind blew hot in the weedy main street, and there was no way to tell that anyone had been here any more recently than ten years previous.

Clint rode the whole length of the main street first, just to be sure there weren't some horses picketed, and then swung down in front of the saloon where the previous night he'd met the messenger from Griego.

He could hear the roar of bluebottles before he even stepped in. The Mexican messenger, soaked with blood, lay where he'd fallen. Clint stirred the flies up considerably rolling the body over and checking the pockets. There was nothing, not even makings. The ammunition and weapons had been taken, the wad of bills was gone.

Clint cleared out and looked for a shovel and a good spot of ground in the small boot hill. Later, sweated up some and needing a sip from his canteen, he took a rest. Then he dragged the messenger's body, and afterwards the body of the other Mexican, to the hole and over the edge. He was not good at saying things over graves, and he had no desire to kick his heels any longer in the desolate wastes of Dead Flats. He mounted White Socks and swung off towards Crooked Creek.

Crooked Creek was a rambunctious kind of a town. There was no marshal or law of any kind, and the folks there seemed to like it that way just fine. It was every man for himself. Boot Hill was filling up rapidly, was soon going to need room to spread itself. Clint had grown tired of towns like this, having seen more of them than most men had, on account of all his wandering. With minor differences they were all the same. Loud, stale, wild, and dangerous. This one was far enough from the wooded lower slopes of the mountains that there were only three wooden buildings. The rest were wind-flapped tents, with a few adobe or stone-and-adobe buildings scattered in. One of the wooden buildings was called the King's Arms Hotel, and was run by a mustached Englishman by the name of Kent. He had a booming laugh and was always coming out with an 'I say, old chap!' or a 'Cheerio,' and his establishment was universally known therefore as Old Chap's Flea Circus, shortened mostly to Chap's. It was here that Clint had stayed the last time he was in town, two nights ago, and there being no better place, he checked in again.

That evening he decided to spend drifting from saloon to saloon with the idea he might hear something or even catch up with the Mexican he'd talked to and retrieved White Socks from. It was his guess that if the Mexican had come to town, word would quickly get around that he was flashing double eagles.

But if it was so, he never heard about it. Maybe even Mexicans around here were flush. He wound up back at Chap's tired and ready to sack out, with nothing to show for his efforts but a pocketful of toothpicks.

But sometime in the night he was awakened by a fight going on in the next room, which was separated from his by the thinnest kind of wall, which instead of muffling the sound acted more like a drum-head, his room being the drum.

He lay there listening to the grunts and then crashing of glass and the splintering of flimsy furniture, and waiting for it to stop.

It went on.

He rolled over facing the other wall and closed his eyes, trying to sleep in spite of it.

13

But it was no use. He might as well have been trying to sleep next to a stamp mill.

It was quite a ruckus. As near as he could make out, there weren't more than two or three dozen of them in there, along with maybe a few steers and a bull that kept bellowing and snorting. Every once in a while somebody would fetch up against the wall and rattle the boards it was made of like cornstalks in the wind, and the whole building would shift sideways, then settle back gingerly, like a sick horse getting kicked. Clint had a pretty certain notion that the boards wouldn't take but only so much, and pretty soon the bull or one of the steers was going to come through and land in his bed.

Clint counted to ten, then reached his gun from under the pillow, ripped back the covers, bounded from the bed, and yanked open the door to the hall. Gun by the barrel, he kicked open the door of the room where the party was going on, and strode in.

Any lights they may have had on were long since smashed, so it was black as the far side of hell and no safer. But Clint was in no mood to concern himself about safety or such a small thing as lack of visibility. He caught an elbow in the jaw and grabbed it with his left hand while with the gun in his right he buffaloed the owner. The man went slack and Clint immediately forgot him and waded further into the fight.

Something hard glanced off his forehead, and he reeled, but only for a moment. The next moment he had the owner of the hard knuckled fist where he wanted him—at his feet on the floor.

This seemed to have considerably quieted the room. In fact, upon stopping to listen, he realized that the fight was over and the distant background sounds of shouting and shooting from the saloons and street was all that was left—peaceful as a church.

Still not having quite finished venting his irritation, he hefted the pistol in his hand, peering around trying to make out if he was the only one left standing, or whether the other party or parties were just holding still.

A scuffle, and then running footfalls as somebody darted out into the hall, only dimly lit by light coming in the window from the street.

Clint went after him, and against the window saw a bulky form, not very tall, in a big hurry. At the head of the rickety staircase, Clint plowed into the man, and they went pinwheeling together down the stairs.

★　　　★　　　★

Clint shook the cobwebs out of his head, then found they weren't quite gone and tried again, then gave it up and very carefully stood to see if everything still worked. As far as he could tell, everything did, except his eyes, which were a bit blurry.

There was a lantern hanging by the desk, but nobody behind the desk. The ruckus obviously hadn't greatly disconcerted anyone. Clint looked around and saw the fat man just coming around, shaking his head back and forth on his thick neck.

Clint squinted down at the man, peering hard through the blur. Didn't he know this man from somewhere? As his vision cleared, he became sure that he'd never seen the face before, and yet there was something about the man . . .

The fat man looked up at him and then brought up his hand feebly.

'Oh, señor,' he moaned. 'Please, señor. Have compassion.'

'Well, I'll be jiggered,' Clint said. 'If it isn't the fat horse-thieving sheepherder. And talking el Inglés too.'

The fat man's eyes widened in surprise, then a look of horror came over him.

'Oh, señor,' he said. 'Please, señor. Have compassion.'

Clint, who still had his clothes on, having

16

acquired the habit long since of sleeping in them so as to be ready for just such fateful encounters as this, patted his pockets and came up with a toothpick. He stuck it in the left corner of his mouth and his lips tipped it skyward.

'Come along, Fats. We're going to have a little talk about compassion.'

CHAPTER THREE

Clint sat him down on the edge of the bed in the room where the fun had taken place. He hunted up a lantern from his own room, lit it, and stood it in the middle of the floor, since the rickety dresser had been tipped over and smashed flat, as had the three chairs and the card table. Cards were strewn everywhere, along with some money—twenty dollar gold pieces, quarters, eagles, gold and silver dollars, and so on. Amongst it all lay the two men Clint had buffaloed. They were still out. One looked like a professional gambler, the other might have been a drifter.

'Now then,' Clint said, propping himself against a wall, looking steadily at the fat Mexican. 'First of all, what was this all about?'

'The fight, señor?' The Mexican's eyes were round and gravely innocent.

'Somebody pulling cards out of his sleeve? Like you, for instance?'

'No, no, señor,' the Mexican protested, waving his arms and rotating his head on his thick neck emphatically. 'It is éstos norteamericanos. They are bad, señor, very bad. They wished to cheat me of my money.'

'Well, it doesn't make a difference to me. You got a pocketful of double eagles. I want them.'

The Mexican feigned exaggerated surprise. 'I have only a small amount of money, señor. And these men wished to take it from me by cheating. I am forever in your debt, señor. You have saved a poor man from becoming even poorer.'

'The way to keep from getting poorer is to stay away from the cards. Let's see the money.'

'It is but a small amount señor . . .'

'Let's see it.'

The Mexican stuffed his chubby hand into a pocket and began groping. He groped for a long while.

With two long strides, Clint was at the Mexican's side, and pulling the hand out. Twenty dollar gold pieces cascaded over the bed and floor.

The toothpick in Clint's mouth tipped up as his jaw took a set. He gathered up the double eagles and jingled them in his big hand. He was about to begin counting the money when the drifter type began to stir.

Soon after, the gambler began to stir as well, and Clint eyed them balefully. He had them sit against the wall a few feet from each other.

'I want some names,' Clint said. 'Starting with you,' he added, leveling a forefinger at the drifter type.

'Wilson. Nick Wilson,' the man said groggily. 'You the one buffaloed me?'

'I'm the fellow. How about you, tinhorn? You got a handle?'

The seedy fellow was looking glumly at his seedy suit, which was torn. 'Red River Thompson.'

'Long way from your territory, aren't you?'

'I just drift around a lot. Never cared for stayin' in one place. What's your angle, mister?'

'I don't like noise when I'm trying to sleep. You Mex, what's your name?'

'I am called Felipe López Francisco Gonzáles, señor.'

'Okay, Thompson. You know this Felipe Fats?'

'I never seen him before tonight.'

'I can guess right easy how it is you happened to be playing poker with him.' Clint jingled the handful of coins. 'How about you, Wilson?'

'I just dropped in for a game with these fellows. I never seen none of them before.'

'I'll wager you always just happen to drop in on Thompson's poker games. Well, just clear out, the both of you.'

'This is my room,' Thompson said, rubbing the lump on his head gingerly.

'Go sleep in the livery or some place. I don't figure to spend all night listening to the way you play poker.'

The two men got up with extreme care and gathered up the cards and the money scattered on the floor.

'But that is my money,' Felipe said.

'The *hell* it is,' said Thompson.

'I reckon you've got plenty without it,' Clint told Felipe. 'Let them have it.'

In a few moments the two men left, and Clint eyed Felipe icily.

'Okay, Mr. Felipe Fats, I know where you got the money, but I don't know what you were doing in Dead Flats in the first place.'

'Señor, I am a poor sheepherder. Pedro—he is my cousin—he say a man has a strong desire for us to go to Dead Flats and watch for you to arrive. Pedro he does not tell me any more.

20

We go to the Dead Flats and Pedro says watch the horses. Then I hear guns, and then a little later, more guns, and then I see you. That is all I know, señor. I swear on my mother's holy grave. I know nothing more at all, señor. Nothing.'

Clint shook the fistful of double eagles under Felipe's nose. 'Just like you know nothing about this money?'

'Señor,' Felipe protested. 'Have compassion. I am a poor man. The money was there. Would you not have taken it yourself?'

'Well, never mind about that. Felipe Fats, I want to know just one thing from you. Where can I find Blake Dixon?'

Felipe's thin dark eyebrows went up expressively. 'I do not know this man, señor.'

'No? You do not know Garcia Valenzuela?'

Felipe became animated, waving his arms. 'I have never heard of him, señor. I know nothing at all. Nothing. I am only a poor sheepherder.'

'Worth about six, seven hundred dollars. Do you know that the man your friend Pedro . . .'

'He is my cousin . . .'

'Whatever. The man he shot was about to give me that money to do something for him. You know what he wanted me to do?'

'I tell you over and over again, señor, until I

21

am very weary of it, that I know nothing. I am completely in the obscure about it.'

'He wanted me to kill two men, by the names of Pedro and Felipe,' Clint said, squinting hard down at the Mexican. 'I have here in my hand the payment for the job. I am known for doing what I'm paid for. I need the money too. Can you think of a good reason why I shouldn't kill you right now and be done with it?'

Felipe's eyes widened, revealing a lot of the whites.

'But señor,' he said. 'It cannot possibly be. Antonio . . .'

'Ah!' Clint pounced. 'Antonio! Now who is Antonio?'

Felipe looked cornered.

'Señor, you have tricked me,' he said aggrievedly. 'I am only a poor sheepherder.'

'Shut up about that sheepherder business. I hear it one more time, I'll plop a few blue whistlers into your mouth—medicinal for what ails you. Now, who is Antonio?'

'He is the man Pedro killed. He is not a good man. He is no loss. Do not cry over him, señor.'

'I won't. What I want to know is where I can find Blake Dixon.'

'But I have told you. I do not know this man.'

Clint drew out the letter, waved it under Felipe's nose.

'From Blake Dixon to Garcia Valenzuela. You and Pedro were working for Valenzuela, that's plain enough. You didn't want Antonio talking to me, hiring me on to find Griego's daughter—don't tell me you know nothing about all this. I don't care about any of it. I don't want to get mixed up in it. If you Mexicans want to kidnap each other's daughters and then have a feud about it, it's nothing to me. I've got my own problems. What I want is Blake Dixon. Now where is he?'

Felipe took the letter and looked at it blankly. 'I have not reading, señor. What does it say?'

Clint told him.

'I know nothing about this,' Felipe said. 'Perhaps Pedro knew where to find Dixon, but I have never even heard of him before.'

'You are no good to me unless you can take me to Dixon,' Clint said. 'You want to die?'

'Oh, señor, have compassion. I cannot help you. It will do no good to kill me. Is not lead expensive? You do not have any good reason to waste lead on me.'

'Sure I do. Think of the satisfaction I will get after the trouble you've caused me.'

'I wish to help, señor. It is only that I

23

cannot. Perhaps if you ask me in the morning, I will think of some way to help you.'

Clint was tired. He scratched his chin.

'Let's have the letter,' he said.

Felipe handed it back, and Clint put it back in his pocket.

'Lie down,' Clint instructed.

He tied Felipe to the bed against the Mexican's protests that it was unnecessary, and then put out the lantern.

'See you at sunup, Felipe Fats,' Clint said, and went out.

Clint lay down on the bed in his own room and closed his eyes. From beyond the wall he could hear Felipe muttering to himself in Spanish. Clint kept thinking about Felipe, but he couldn't make up his mind if Felipe knew anything about Dixon or not.

CHAPTER FOUR

At first light, Clint was up. He went out and bought breakfast in an open air feed bin known as Dora's. The food was not bad, a bit undercooked. Afterwards he returned to the hotel and entered Felipe's room. The fat Mexican looked up at him with the expression of a patient much-maligned dog.

'Señor,' he said. 'It is very uncomfortable.'

Clint untied Felipe and then watched as Felipe sat up and rubbed his limbs, groaning and moaning.

'Perhaps you have decided you would like to help,' Clint suggested.

'Señor,' Felipe said, 'I have been thinking. This Señor Dixon. He is a friend of yours?' When Clint didn't do more than shrug, Felipe went on. 'I seem to record something Pedro said about this man the Señor Dixon. It is possible I could lead you to him. But I am not sure.'

'Ah,' Clint said, and waited.

'I have a very big family,' Felipe said. 'I am very poor. My wife, she is very seek, you know? And there are so many little ones. It is almost impossible to feed them all, you know?'

'If you want to be around to take care of them, take me to Dixon.'

'Señor, I may be wrong. I am not sure. It is a long way. Think what may happen to my family while I am away! When I return, they will be even poorer than before.'

'You take me to Dixon, and then maybe I'll feel like passing out money. We'll see.'

'We will need burros. It is a long trip. We will need supplies.'

'Then I'll buy them. How long a trip?'

25

'A week, two weeks. It is a long way, señor.'

'Then let's get at it.'

*　　　*　　　*

It took most of the day to round up the necessary burros and the necessary supplies. Clint hated the notion of using burros, but good pack horses were impossible to find. They got into a heated discussion more than once about food. Clint had in mind dried beans, fresh apples, coffee, sugar, malt, yeast and flour, the last four for making sourdough bisquits. But Felipe insisted on sacks of corn for making tortillas and especially a whole range of herbs and spices, though mostly chili peppers. And he wanted to bring a staggering supply of tequila. Clint didn't mind some whiskey, so long as it was something more than creosote and alcohol, but he didn't want Felipe drunk all the time. Clint didn't even mind a few tortillas once in a while, or some chili, so long as they were not too hot, but he was not about to spend the next month or so living on nothing but those things. He'd heard eating too much Mexican food will make your tongue so leathery you'd never taste any other food again.

It was nearly sundown when they were

finally ready to load the burros, having about twice the amount of food they really needed, and a great irritation with each other. They spent one more night in the hotel, Clint tying the Mexican to his bed again, so he could get a good night's sleep without worrying about what Felipe was up to.

★   ★   ★

As the sun began to beat down on the constant bedlam of Crooked Creek, Clint Evans, toothpick jutting from the corner of his mouth, and Felipe López Francisco González, known to Clint as Felipe Fats, rode out of town, going west. Clint was aboard White Socks, Felipe aboard his own scrawny horse. Before they started, Felipe drank some tequila for breakfast. Clint eyed the jugs of it on the pack of one of the burros and wondered if he had allowed Felipe too large a ration.

At noon, sweating in the sun, they stopped in a small canyon, and tried to crowd into the shade of an overhang. They drank water, then tequila, and while Clint ate an apple and made cryptic remarks, Felipe started a fire, kneaded maize and cooked himself a tortilla, liberally spiced, on a flat rock in the fire. Felipe sweated a lot over it, the drippings spitting in the fire.

27

'You're going to use up our water twice as fast that way, Fats,' Clint said. 'What's the matter with an apple?'

'I always eat a good meal in the middle of the day, you know? It is good for the soul and good for the body.'

'You're liable to burn them both out before you ever get to hell, setting by a fire in the sun in the middle of the day.'

An hour after they started moving again, they came on a brush hut, about ten by fifteen, roof of thatched leaves, with three small boys asleep beside the door, sombreros tipped down over their eyes.

'Thees is my home,' Felipe said. 'I must say goodbye to Adelita and los hijos.'

Clint went into the hovel with Felipe mostly just to get out of the sun. A goat came over and began chewing at his pant leg. There was also a turkey, a couple of pigs, a dog. No furniture. A worn out looking woman with many teeth missing sat in the middle of the floor grinding maize into powder in a stone bowl. Straw sleeping mats were rolled up at one side. A couple more children, both girls, were weaving a new mat.

In rapid Spanish, Felipe told his wife about Pedro's death, and that he was in the hire of the norteamericano to help him find a man called Blake Dixon, and that he would be back in a short while, that it would be a jornado only, meaning a small chore, a day's journey. It was only a figure of speech. He told her he didn't know exactly how long he would be gone, but that he hoped it would not be too long. He asked her how she was, was she feeling better? She told him she hoped the norteamericano was going to pay well, and he said she was not to worry. She looked hard at Clint as though she wanted to give him a piece of her mind.

Shortly afterward they left, now going almost due north.

'You work for Valenzuela, and he doesn't even pay you enough that you can afford to move out of that hovel?' Clint asked as they rode along.

'I do not work for Valenzuela for money. He is a cousin. One does favors for cousins.'

'I see. Pedro was his cousin too, then?'

'Sí. We are all cousins.'

'But he doesn't pay you anything. He expects you to go around killing people just because you're family?'

'I did not say he does not pay. Of course he pays. This is how I afford a horse and tequila. But it is not the reason why I do it.'

They rode on a while in silence. Clint adjusted his bandana to cover the back of his neck more thoroughly.

29

'I will pay you what is left of the money Antonio was supposed to hire me with if you will do everything you can to help me find Dixon and cause me no trouble.'

Felipe's eyes shone, since even after buying the burros and the supplies there was a substantial amount of money left.

'That means you don't lead me on a wild goose chase or run off in the night. Agreed?'

'Sí, señor. Sí.'

'If it all works out the way I hope, I won't need the burros either, and you can have them.'

'Oh, señor, it is too much! Muchas Gracias!'

'But I don't want trouble. Is that clear? I'm paying you that so you will not decide your cousin may want you and ride off. You got that straight?'

'Oh, señor. I have it very straight! I give you my word on my mother's holy grave.'

'Never mind your mother's holy grave.'

*   *   *

That night, as the sky turned crimson, with the sun burning in big flames just over the edge of the empty desert, they made camp twenty paces from a broken down Concord coach that was sunk hub deep in sand and had the lettering mostly worn off from the drilling of blowing grit. Clint started the fire while Felipe hobbled the horses and burros. Clint made sourdough bisquits and beans and coffee. When Felipe returned from the chores with the animals, he was still beaming with joy and pleasure, but when he saw the food, the corners of his mouth went down.

'Try some,' Clint invited. 'This here is real food.'

But Felipe had a hard time with it. He tried valiantly and actually got some of it down as Clint had cooked it, but in the end he waited until Clint had had his fill of the beans, and then added some chili and various other herbs. Then he was able to smile again as he ate. He drank tequila, a lot, but it didn't seem to bother him much.

The red in the sky got lower and lower as the blue turned purple and then black and filled with stars.

'It is very beautiful here, no?' Felipe said softly. And then he began to sing. Clint listened and remembered a Jew's harp his father used to play, many years ago, back in the woods camps in various places in New England.

Soon they turned in and Clint, depending on the lure of money to hold Felipe, and on a lariat to keep away diamondbacks and

31

sidewinners, closed his eyes and went peacefully to sleep . . .

He smelled chili. He opened his eyes and bending over him was Felipe.

CHAPTER FIVE

What was more, one of Felipe's pudgy hands was trying to get into Clint's money-carrying pocket.

Clint came up off the ground as though he'd suddenly discovered he'd been lying on a cactus. Turning his head from the nauseous cloud of Felipe's chili-heavy breath, Clint pushed the Mexican over onto his back, trying to pin the thick arms.

'Oh, señor,' Felipe gasped, still struggling. 'Please, señor . . .'

Clint, straddling Felipe's belly, having failed to pin the flailing arms, straightened up, hauled off and belted Felipe across the jaw just so. Felipe's arms flopped down lifelessly and the struggle was over.

Clint slowly got off Felipe and sat down to one side.

'Damned Mexicans,' he muttered, very irritated. 'I should have known.'

When Felipe came around, Clint had

finished tying him up and was back in his blanket roll, eyes closed, trying to get back to sleep.

'Oh, señor,' Felipe said. 'I am sorry. But I think I hear something.'

'I don't want to hear your lies. I trusted you, but that was not too smart. I should have known better than to trust a Mexican. Now shut up, or I'll have to crowd your handkerchief down your throat to stopper you off.'

'Please, señor. I am not lying. Suppose somebody wants to kill us? That would be bad, no?'

Clint wondered if he could have been mistaken about where Felipe's hand was, decided he was not mistaken, and said, 'I won't give you an more warnings.'

Felipe sighed heavily and aggrievedly, and was silent.

*　　　*　　　*

When the sun came up, the horses were cropping a patch of grass not far off, but the burros were nowhere to be seen.

After the previous night's disappointment with Felipe, which caused the further irritation of disturbed sleep, Clint was not in a good mood to begin with. The disappearance

33

of the mules soured him still more.

'Dad blamed burros,' he muttered. 'Wish to hell we could have found some pack horses instead. Come on, Fats, we've got to go looking.'

It took them half the morning to find the burros, pack up and get ready to leave. By that time, Clint had recalled the story of the old miner who'd been fifty years panning gold in the mountains—and spent thirty of them hunting his burros.

Clint was also wondering if there wasn't some easier way to get to Blake Dixon than this. But he didn't come up with one.

All day, an argument went on between them.

'But señor, this is the country of Mescaleros,' Felipe said. 'If I am tied up, I am not able to fight.'

'You had your chance. But you damned Mexicans are all alike. Here I was trying to do you a good turn, and what do you do? Why, you try to steal the money and take off. You're a thief, nothing more, Fats. If I didn't need you to take me to Dixon, I'd turn you loose and be shut of you.'

'Señor, it is all a misunderstanding, so unfortunate. I was merely trying to wake you . . .'

'Aw, put the cork in, will you, Fats? You

get on my nerves lying the same lie at me over and over.'

'But señor, it is no lie . . .'

That night, Clint had to listen to several more rounds of the same conversation as he bound Felipe's ankles and wrists. He was still in a bad mood, two of the burros having been obstinate all day, in addition to the way Felipe wore at him like a tight pair of boots. They had cooked separate meals, but the air was perversely still around camp for a change, and the heavy smell of chili and God only knew what else pervaded the atmosphere. Clint went to sleep hoping the tighter hobbles he'd put on the burros would keep them closer by, so that at least tomorrow it would be possible to get off to a reasonably early start.

Something was moving out there in the night. Something that only just barely stirred the blow sand. Clint sat up and peered around, rifle in one hand, pistol in the other.

He heard nothing. The air was still.

For some time he listened, still hearing nothing, and then he decided to take a look around, perhaps check on the horses and burros, and then go back to sleep.

The burros were not where he'd left them, nor were they within a radius of two hundred yards of where he'd left them, as far as he could tell. He cursed, but figured that was about all he could do until first light. He was about to get back into his roll, when he heard Felipe's whisper.

'Señor?'

'What?'

'I am sure I hear something. While you are gone. It is Mescalero, Señor, I am sure of it. This is their country, señor. It is very dangerous here.'

'Indians won't fight at night, at least not Mescaleros. Don't you know that?'

'Sí, señor. But steel I hear something.'

'So'd I, but it's probably just a night critter. Now shut up and let me sleep.'

'I think you should untie me, señor. If there is someone out there . . .'

'There isn't. I just checked.'

'But señor.'

'Shut up, Fats, and go to sleep.'

'Señor, please'

Clint closed his eyes and willed himself to go to sleep. But it wouldn't come. He pictured the mesquite bushes full of Apaches, waiting for morning. He remembered numerous stories about Indian raids and of discovery of bones bleaching in the sun. He recalled stories of torture and slow death, and could already hear the wild calls the Mescaleros would make come morning.

He got up and untied Felipe.

36

'Oh, señor, I am so grateful. It is much wiser this way. This way we will be ready for them.'

'I'll be ready for you, too, remember. Don't get any notions.

'Please, señor, do not fear. I never wished to harm you.'

'I'm thinking of what you might try to steal and then ride off with.'

'But señor, I would not steal from you. I have told you this so many times. Why do you not believe me?'

They got no more sleep that night, digging a ditch to fight from, burying their supplies, watching for Mescaleros. At the first graying of the eastern sky, they stopped talking—it had not been a very fruitful or enlightening conversation in any case—and became tense, watching and listening. Felipe started to drink tequila, but Clint made him put it away.

Now the wind picked up, rustling dryly in the brush, tickling the blow sand idly this way and that. There were other small sounds, each of which made them both jump.

The sun suddenly lifted its rim over the eastern horizon, throwing fiery light across the desert. And abruptly a terrible scream went up somewhere to the east of them, and the mesquite shook as Indians came plunging through them, brandishing a motley assortment of pistols, rifles and knives.

'Por Dios!' Felipe said.

The end of the well-chewed toothpick in Clint's mouth tipped up. He slammed the butt of his Winchester against his shoulder and began shooting. Three wild and fierce screaming Indians puffed dust and skidded to a halt. But four more stepped over them without a break in stride and came on.

'Señor, they are behind!' yelled Felipe, and shot at the attackers opening up from the other direction.

With bullets coming at them from both directions, sticking their heads above the edge of the small ditch they'd dug was no more comfortable then sticking them into a hornets' nest.

After the first few shots from behind, the air was full of smoke, which drifted lazily towards them on the breeze. It was a lucky thing, since it provided cover.

A couple of Indians got through the wall of bullets Clint was putting up, and knives flashed dimly in the sun-brightened smoke. Clint swung the butt of his Winchester and knocked one Indian into the other. As they stumbled briefly, Clint got the gun turned business end out again and finished them off with a couple of shots.

But by now three more Indians had plunged

through the fog of smoke and one had got Felipe by the hair and was going for the fat throat with a long, bone-handled knife. Clint at that moment discovered he was out of bullets and dropped the Winchester and drew and fired his Colt with one smooth motion. Felipe's attacker jolted sideways, dropping his knife and slumping into the sand. Clint plowed lead into the other two Indians a fraction of a second later, and then there was suddenly only the ringing of his ears.

The smoke cleared. The only Indians in sight were dead Indians.

'Ees all over, señor,' Felipe sighed. 'They have given up.'

'They'll try again, you can bet,' Clint said. 'Let's find those burros, if the Indians haven't stolen them. We'll go together, and watch each other's backs.'

They were most of the morning finding the burros, having to track them through aimless wanderings. But, though he and Felipe both looked very carefully, they did not see any sign of Indians.

They returned to camp, dug up their packs, loaded the burros and set off. Still they had seen nothing more of the Indians.

'They are out there, señor,' Felipe said softly. 'They are waiting and following.'

'I'm surprised they didn't attack again.

Maybe we killed them all.'

'No, señor, I do not think so. They are waiting for a good time. They have places of bad medicine. Perhaps we are crossing such a place now, and when we come out the other side . . .'

'Could be right, I guess. But just keep your eyes peeled, this is risky, travelling, if they're going to attack again. I'm counting on them waiting for another early morning. Anyway, we can't afford to try to wait them out holed up in the middle of nowhere.'

'Sí, señor. My eyes are peeled very much. Señor, I am so very grateful to you. You saved my life, señor. I have much gratitude.'

'I should have let him slit your throat,' Clint muttered.

They saw nothing of Indians or anyone else all day. They made camp in a lone pile of rocks, this time tying up the horses and burros to a spire of rock. There was nothing for the animals to feed on here, but Clint was worried that the Indians might make off with them.

After cooking supper—two suppers actually—Clint was presented with the problem once again of whether to tie up Felipe. If he did, it could be risky. If he did not, Felipe might slip away.

'You won't live long if you try to take off in the night,' Clint said.

'I know that, señor.'

'I'll wake up if you try anything.'

'I know that, señor.'

'There are only two reasons I don't slit your throat myself and be done with it. I need you to find Blake Dixon. And I need you to help me fight Mescaleros.'

'I know that, señor.'

'And there's only one reason for not tying you up tonight. You know what that is, Fats.'

'I know, señor.'

'It won't do you any good to try anything. If I don't get you, the Indians will.'

'I am sure, señor.'

'I don't care a cow flat for your word, Fats. It's no good. I am not depending on your word. I'm depending on your desire to stay alive. The only way that will happen is if we stay together and work together. Is that clear?'

'It is very clear,' Felipe said patiently. 'Señor, I really do have much gratitude to you for saving my life. I will not forget it soon, señor.'

'Save it, Fats.'

'Goodnight, señor.'

'Do you always have to say señor? The handle's just Clint.'

'If you wish, señor—dispense usted, *Cleent*.'

'Clint.'

41

'Si, señor. Cleent.'
'Oh the hell with it.'

CHAPTER SIX

Well before dawn, Clint was sitting in a handy spot in the rocks watching the desert in all directions. He had heard nothing, seen nothing. The wind was light, just enough to feel cool against his face. At least Felipe had not attempted anything. He was now busy checking the loads in his battered old pistol and Winchester.

As the sky in the east brightened, Felipe took up a position in the rocks facing the west, leaving Clint to concentrate on the east. They waited.

The day peered at them over the horizon, then quickly flooded the arid wastes with harsh gold light.

Clint, everpresent toothpick in mouth, watched with squinted hard eyes for the mesquite to start thrashing with Indians.

But the sun lifted full above the horizon, and no Indians. The sun heated the rock so it was hot to the touch, and still no Indians.

'I think we killed them all back there,' Clint said, standing up and stretching.

'I do not think so, Cleent. They are out there, waiting.'

'Well, we can't wait any longer. Let's eat something and get out of here.'

Breakfast was a nervous affair. For Felipe it was nervous because he remained convinced that the Indians were still about to attack. For Clint it was nervous because Felipe kept getting up and peering from the rocks into the desert, and muttering doubtfully in Spanish.

After breakfast, they saddled the horses, slung the packs on the burros and cleared out. The sun was hot, the wind strong enough to be gritty, and Felipe was still very nervous. Clint felt more relaxed now. He had about convinced himself that they'd either killed all the Indians or had driven them off for good, and he was thinking now about Blake Dixon and about Margaret lying naked and battered in the woods. Dixon was going to pay dearly for his fun. He imagined himself cutting Dixon up with his knife, and grinned thinking of how Dixon would writhe and holler with pain.

Not having had to round up the burros had gotten them off to a good start, and at first they made good time. Clint was pleased. Felipe, however, still could not forget the Indians. Clint poked fun at Felipe, enjoying himself.

43

'*What's that, Fats?*' he would say suddenly, and Felipe would jerk around and say, 'Where, Cleent?' Clint would shrug and say, 'You missed it. I thought you might know what kind of bird that was.' Then he would hoot at the sky and slap his knee. It worked three times in a row before Felipe quit jumping.

'Cleent, you are making a joke, but it is no joke,' Felipe said finally. He was sweating heavily. 'It is not funny.'

'Ees not funny? Eh? Oh, Señor Felipe Fats López Francisco González Tortilla, I am so sorry you do not enjoy thee joke!'

'Cleent, I have much patience. But I do not like to be made fun of.'

'I don't care for lying thieves either,' Clint said. But he felt lighthearted and had gotten to the point where he didn't much care what Felipe was or wasn't. He figured he had it all under control now. He could manage Felipe as long as he had to, and get done with Blake Dixon. Then, well, then he could leave the fat Mexican to his tortillas and tequila.

Sometime before noon, the day's troubles started. The burros, obstinate and ornery under the best conditions, were working with no night's grazing in their bellies. After a hot morning they lost interest in moving along when they came on a scrawny patch of grass that was better than the usual run. They halted and began to eat, ignoring the tugs in the lead ropes.

'Dad blamed burros,' Clint said. 'Keep tugging, Fats. I'm going to cut a switch.'

'Cleent, it will do no good. The burros are hungry. The only thing to do is let them eat.'

'Just keep the tension on.'

'Sí, I will do that, Cleent. But it will do no good, I am telling you.'

Clint cut a switch of thorny mesquite and set to work on the rump of the aftermost burro. The animal flinched ahead a few paces and then went back to cropping grass. Clint flailed some more, and the burro repeated the performance, ending up to one side of the next burro. Clint, now sweating wet as standing in a rainstorm, beat first one, then the other of these two burros, moving them up even with the third one. Then he worked on all three. They progressed in this way to the edge of the grass. But here the pattern changed. Instead of jerking ahead, the burros went to one side or just turned around, or sometimes kicked, refusing absolutely to leave the patch of grass, just as though there was a fence around it.

'Cleent, Cleent, heet that one! No no, *that* one. Watch out behind, Cleent! That one will keek you! No, Cleent, not *that* one. *That* one . . . Por Dios, Cleent, can you not make them go at all?'

Clint quit, throwing the switch off into the brush, irritated at Felipe. Felipe was about to fall off his horse with laughter.

'Think it's Goddamned funny, do you Fats?' Clint shouted, clenching his fists. 'I ought to take you down a peg, you fat thieving lying Mexican tortilla chili bean. I ought to make a Mexican *jumping* bean out of you, eh?'

Felipe was hooting with laughter, thin black mustache stretched even thinner. Clint charged him, but Felipe wheeled his horse and rode in circles around Clint, waving his sombrero over his head and laughing. Clint stood helplessly in the dust and yelled obscenities.

*   *   *

'Guess I had it coming,' Clint admitted, as they sat in the shade of a patch of mesquite watching the horses and burros graze. The apples were gone, but Clint had some sourdough bisquits left from the previous night and he ate them slowly, making them last. Felipe had insisted on cooking a tortilla on a flat rock in a fire in the hot sun. Now he was guzzling tequila and munching the tortilla, rolled up with some godless spices inside.

'Let us be friends, Cleent. Let us trust each other.'

Clint looked carefully at the Mexican. He sure looked genuine about it. If Clint had not had that bad experience waking up in the night to find Felipe fishing his pockets for the money, he would have taken Felipe at his word.

Could it be he was mistaken? The whole event tended to fade into an obscure darkness. Could Felipe have really been telling the truth? Was it possible?

Clint wasn't sure now. He still tended to mistrust Felipe. But when a man has fought for his life with another man at his side, even gone so far as to save the man's life, he tended to trust his companion. In this case, it might not be such a smart thing to do. Felipe had sided him out of the same necessity Clint had sided the Mexican: survival. Neither of them could expect to survive alone against the Indians. It was unlikely good luck that they'd survived as only two against the Indians.

Yet the feeling remained.

'What the hell,' Clint said, throwing his better judgement to the winds.

'Sí, Cleent,' Felipe said, grinning broadly, 'what thee hell!'

'I don't like that grin,' Clint said dubiously. 'But like I said, what the hell.'

'You will not be sorry, Cleent. I am your friend for life because I have much gratitude. You are a fine man, Cleent. You don't like people to think you are fine, but I have the sharp eyes and ears, no? I can see.'

'I still don't like that grin of yours. I . . .' Clint broke off, catching sight of something out in the desert. He jumped up, rifle in hand. 'Sonofabitch,' he said, and started running towards the burros.

Several Mescaleros were cutting the packs off the burros—they were smart enough not to try to take the burros along too. Clint and Felipe shouldered their Winchesters and started spitting lead at the Indians.

That had the effect of triggering a barrage of fire and smoke from the mesquite thicket behind them. With lead buzzing the air around them, they both dove with alacrity into the nearest cover, which happened to be another clump of mesquite, thick and thorny. It was not a comfortable dive into the middle of the thorns, but it was better than braving the bullets.

As soon as they were neatly cornered in the mesquite, the Indians quit wasting their lead. The smoke blew away, and there was no way to tell the Indians were still there. But the point was, you knew they *were* still there.

Out on the patch of grass, Indians, perhaps

twenty of them, were quickly dividing up the spoils. It didn't take long. They didn't even leave the aparejos, though what good they were without the burros was hard to see. Perhaps they figured to sell them, or use the leather in them. The Mescaleros rode off taking the two horses but wisely leaving the burros.

Clint had meanwhile been trying to struggle his rifle around through the thick thorny brush to get a shot at the Mescaleros. Now, finally, he managed it, sent a few shots after the retreating Indians, got a few parting shots in return, and then the Indians, including those which had been in the mesquite, were gone in a cloud of dust that grew smaller and smaller.

Clint and Felipe struggled out of the thorn bushes and leaned on their Winchesters.

'Goddamned Indians,' Clint said. '*Tricky* sons of guns, *aren't* they? Well damnit, we can't let them get away with that. That was all our supplies, our water, except for a canteen apiece.'

'All the tequila,' Felipe moaned. 'Cleent, we cannot go after them. It will be stupid. And we will never catch them anyhow. No, Cleent, we are just the misfortunates. It is the way the world passes, no? There is nothing we can do.'

But Clint was angry. He had made up his mind the Indians weren't going to get away with this, never mind there were twenty-five or thirty of them, armed to the teeth and with a terrifying reputation for fighting and torture. It did not cross his mind that perhaps he and Felipe had been lucky to have kept their lives, under the circumstances.

He trotted to the burros, swung aboard one, and using the lead line for reins, dug in his heels. The burro was not particularly impressed. It went on cropping grass.

'Get up!' Clint instructed. 'Get along you damnfool critter.'

The burro's long ears perked around interestedly, but the animal went on cropping grass.

'Arre! Burro! Arre!' Clint shouted, remembering the way Felipe talked to the burros. The burro was still not impressed, though the ears kept perked around for listening.

'The burro he doesn't want to chase Indians,' Felipe said coming up. 'I think perhaps the burro is smarter than you in this way, Cleent.'

Clint got down and cut a switch. The Indians were completely out of sight over a rise by now, and not even dust marked their position.

Clint got back on the burro and began whaling the animal's flank with the switch, sinking his spurs in and yelling, 'Arre, burro, Arre!'

Felipe folded his arms and watched dolefully.

'El burro, he is muy independiente, no?' he commented.

The burro had not budged. In fact, he had eaten everything within reach and would have to move to go on eating, but did not apparently care to encourage Clint into thinking all his efforts were paying off.

Clint, sweating and swearing now, leaped off this burro and tried another—with the exact same result.

'Cleent, I have the good luck with los burros because I do not try to make them do what they do not wish to do. It is plain they do not wish to chase Indians. I believe they have much sense in so thinking, Cleent. Let us seet down in the shade and think about this while los burros have their lunch, eh?'

Clint was not satisfied. He was worried, and that made him angry.

'I want to know which way they went,' he said, and went running towards the top of the rise, leaving Felipe ambling slowly back to the shade of the mesquite thicket.

Clint, breathing hard and drenched with

sweat, halted on the top of the long rise and gazed around the horizon. There was nothing but sun-drenched desert. Not a puff of dust anywhere. There was another rise probably a mile off, and he debated running over there for a look, but decided against it.

He'd calmed down some now, and had realized that Felipe was right. Clint knew better. In fact, usually he would have kept his head. It was just having Felipe and the burros to contend with . . .

He returned in no haste, taking it easy, trying not to sweat any more than necessary. It was stupid to sweat off more water than he really had to. One canteen had to get him to the next watering hole, wherever that might be.

Felipe was asleep under his sombrero when Clint returned. How can he sleep in this situation? Clint wondered. Clint had always thought of himself as pretty cool most of the time, but here was this Mexican going to sleep first thing after a catastrophe. Maybe he just wasn't smart enough to know better?

No, Felipe was plenty smart enough. He was just cool.

'What did you see, señor Cleent?'

'Nothing.'

'It is good, no? Perhaps the Indians are finished with us, eh?'

'That's what we thought the last time.'

'Sí. They like to kill. I am surprised they did not kill us. Maybe they try again. Perhaps they are in a big hurry for something. There is trail three days east from here, and many wagons go by sometimes. Perhaps they know one is coming, eh? And they will be back for us when they have more time.'

'They do, and I'm going to see not one gets away alive.'

'This will be hard to do. And not wise. It is better that we hide, no? We see them coming and we hide. They will not take the burros, as you see. They know the burros will not move fast enough, and perhaps they will not move at all, eh?' Felipe grinned. 'Perhaps they will shoot them, but that is a risk we take.'

'Funny about you, Felipe,' Clint said. 'Before the Indians scared you, got you all jumpy. Now you are calm. It doesn't make any sense.'

'I was afraid of loss. But now the horses and the supplies they are gone. What is there to be afraid of? You and me, we can hide. We dig ourselves into the sand, it is the old trick. The horses could not hide, and the packs too much time to hide. But now the worst has happened. It is the way the world passes, is it not? There is nothing to be done. Worry will do no good and much harm. Do not fear,

53

Cleent, we will live.'

CHAPTER SEVEN

'You say there's a trail three days to the east of here?'

'Sí. But it will be stupid to go that way if the Mescaleros have gone that way. And it is just the same to the mountains, where we go.'

'Those mountains we've been looking at since we started?'

'Sí. I think it may be that Señor Dixon will be in Oak Creek. I do not make the guarantee, Cleent. It is just a hope.'

'You figure three days?'

'Three or four. Perhaps more. It depends much on los burros.'

'Maybe we can walk it more quickly.'

'Perhaps.'

'What are we going to water the burros with?'

'Los burros will need only what is in our canteens. They will be thirsty, but they will live.'

'Wait a minute. You plan to give all the water to the burros?'

'Sí. It is best. Three days is not long without water.'

'Damn sight longer than I want to go. Suppose it takes five days or longer? If it's a three day ride you can figure the burros will take more like three weeks. In this sun we'll never make it. I think we ought to shoot the damn burros and walk. Then we get there just as fast and we have something to drink along the way.'

'Señor Cleent, have you not been a few days without water before?'

'Once. I don't figure on doing it again.'

'There may be certain cactus with water, if you are uncomfortable.'

'What's the good of saving the burros?'

'Señor, it is a long walk.'

'Let the burros eat cactus.'

'Sometimes they will not. It is not so bad, Cleent. It is better to ride than to walk.'

'I'll tell you what I think. I think you want to save the burros so you can steal them when we get to the mountains, along with the money.'

Felipe waved his arms. 'It is not true, Cleent! Por Dios, it is not true at all. I only wish to ride, not walk. It is a long and painful walk in riding boots, Cleent.'

Clint eyed Felipe dubiously, not convinced at all that Felipe's motive was what he claimed it was. But at the same time, Clint was realizing how much his feet hurt him from the running he'd done in his tight riding boots. They were not made for walking. He imagined walking in them for a week, and reluctantly decided to go along with Felipe.

The burros saw fit to move on after the sun had gotten a good start down the sky. It was not exactly cooler, but the sun's rays had lost some of their fierce furnace-like quality. On Felipe's insistence they watered the burros from their hats.

'Why bother with all three?' Clint demanded. 'Two burros is plenty.'

'It will be better to have one to spare. If they get rests, los burros will go faster.'

'The water will go further with only two animals,' Clint argued.

'The burros will need less water if they work less hard,' Felipe returned.

Clint was very dubious about Felipe's sense of economy, but he did have to admit that Felipe had lived many years in the desert whereas he himself had only been down south here for a couple of years or so, and had never had anything to do with burros before. He was used to real grassland and streams and wooded mountainsides. This lizard and sun country wasn't his kind of thing.

Clint didn't really feel thirsty until they stopped for supper. The burros had not caused undue trouble, though were never in any hurry. Now Clint hobbled them and Felipe insisted they give the animals a small ration of water. They had not passed any of the cactus Felipe had mentioned. He said he did not recall having seen any in this stretch of desert before, but that there might be a stray or two somewhere.

Since there was nothing to eat and nothing to drink, Clint lay down and went to sleep as soon as the burros were taken care of, leaving Felipe on watch. He decided if he slept soundly and Felipe got the money away from him and then took off, well, that was just too bad. As Felipe would say, that was just the way the world passed.

Felipe woke him up, breathing out fumes that still smelled of chili, and Clint took over watch, having checked his pockets and found both the letter and money still there. The sky was huge and the stars brilliant. As the rest of the night went by, he watched them parade west and disappear beyond the horizon.

In the morning, now feeling hungry as well as thirsty, he helped water the burros and then they climbed aboard and rode on.

The burros were now less ambitious and kept stopping to crop grass or sniff at thorn bushes. Felipe took to cries of 'Arre! Burro! Arre!' At noon they took a rest, a long one to pass the heat of the day, with the hope of conserving water and energy. Clint was very tempted to take a sip of water, but figured if Felipe could get along without, he could. Felipe looked subdued, but otherwise unchanged.

The afternoon jaunt was even slower than the morning. Clint estimated at the end of the day that they hadn't made more than ten miles, perhaps less than that. Again they took the night in watches.

The next two days were much the same. The mountains seemed to tower over them, but somehow they didn't appear to get any closer. At least they saw no Indians.

Clint's tongue was swollen by this time, and it hurt to talk. His lips were parched. Just watching the burros slurp up water was painful knowing he couldn't have some himself. And they were pouring away their water to burros yet! If it had been White Socks he wouldn't have minded a bit. But these useless critters were a source of great irritation to him.

Felipe seemed to go on without much change. It was true he spoke very seldom and almost always it was to cry 'Arre!' at the burros, but he seemed to be able to sweat right along, reeking of rancid chili and whatever. Clint wondered if Felipe was taking a sip in the night while on watch, but if he did, it wasn't much, since the levels in the canteens seemed no different as far as he could tell. Felipe couldn't be all that dependent on tequila—at least he showed no effects of being deprived of it.

Clint figured he could last one more day, then he was going to take a drink before the burros had gotten it all. The hell with Felipe and the burros. Let the burros go thirsty for once.

But by the next night they had given all the water to the burros in an effort to make them perk up. However, they were within a short distance of the foothills, and could see the fluffs of cottonwoods along the stream bank. The burros did not want to go on once they'd stopped in the evening for a rest.

'I don't care about the danged burros now,' Clint rasped. 'I'll walk if I have to, but I'm going to get a drink before I sleep.'

'Sí,' Felipe said. 'It is the way I feel also.'

They left the burros and began walking, Clint ignoring the pain his tight riding boots gave him. They hadn't gone far before they noticed the burros walking briskly along behind.

They climbed aboard a couple of the burros and dug in their heels. Now the burros became interested in some grass and would not move.

They swung off again and began walking. And again the burros began following. Clint was too weak to swear, or he'd have made the desert echo with obscenities.

It was close to midnight when they stumbled down the stream bank and discovered . . . mud.

Clint croaked something inarticulate, and Felipe muttered something venomous in Spanish, and they crawled forward over the mud on their hands and knees.

There turned out to be water after all, but only a small sluggish trickle that normally Clint would have turned up his nose at as too brackish. But now it was better than any other water he'd ever tasted.

The burros, with much excited braying, came and plunged in stirring up the mud, kicking their heels and snorting in the water.

That night, Clint slept comfortably, and by tacit agreement they didn't bother to keep watch.

In the morning, the burros were nowhere to be seen.

'Perhaps we should skin them alive, no?' Felipe said.

Clint looked at Felipe in surprise.

'I thought you had a great love for the burros,' he said.

'That was because it was necessary.'

'Funny, I think they're a damned nuisance and I wouldn't own burros as a usual thing, and I've never seen a more ornery obstinate critter than what a burro is, and if a man gave me a choice of burros or paying him ten dollars, I'd pay up and figure I'd got the best of the deal. But you know Felipe, it is a fact that those burros got us here. They didn't do it like horses would have, and they caused us considerable cussing energy and so on, but they *did* get us here, and that's a fact. I guess I've got kind of used to them around and I don't feel like skinning them at all.'

'The trouble with you, Cleent, is you no are practical, you know? You don't like los burros when it is sensible to like them, and you do like them after it becomes unnecessary to like them. It is a big difference between you and me.'

'I guess so. Let's hunt them up.'

It took only an hour, and then they began trying to hurry the animals along towards Oak Creek, suddenly feeling hungry. The burros were not hungry. They had had their fill of water and all they wished to do was roll in the mud and lie in the shade. Felipe coaxed them sweetly, intermingled with cries of 'Arre!' Clint began to think Felipe might have had a good idea after all in skinning them alive.

Towards noon, following the well-worn

61

trail along the creek, they rode into Oak Creek. It was a pleasant, shady little town, a mining town but with the rowdy bloom off, leaving mostly solid citizens and prosperous big mines, which were up a stony face of mountain west of town and looming above it. Mine shaft headings dotted it like tiny dormers, with flimsy threads of chutes down which ore poured to the bottom of the cliff. It gave the town a background roar something like a bunch of waterfalls.

They left their burros with a disdainful livery man who was surprised to find that men who rode burros could afford to pay cash money for livery.

With the burros off their hands, and the Mescaleros left behind somewhere in the desert, Clint felt a great relief. They hunted up two separate eating establishments, since they couldn't find one that served food hot enough to please Felipe and at the same time served food that Clint could think of as edible. Clint gave Felipe enough to pay for his meal and they parted, agreeing to meet in the square where the town's two major roads crossed afterwards.

Clint stoked his furnaces in leisurely fashion, managing to get down some of about everything on the menu and astonishing the round faced woman who served him.

'This town is full of big-eating miners,' she said shaking her head, 'but I never seen nothing like you before.'

Clint grinned and asked for more pie.

He left feeling so full he couldn't bend over, and when he found a bench in the square to sit on, he was careful how he sat, stretching his legs out straight and sitting forward on the seat so he could lean back.

It felt damned good to be doing nothing but sit in the shade for a while, knowing he was perfectly safe from Indians, burros, and the odd notions in Felipe's head.

He sat there for quite a while, eyes closed, letting time go by, listening to the cries of teamsters and the distant rumbling roar of the ore spewing down the rock face. He daydreamed that Felipe was trying to catch the burros and they were shying away from him to eat grass, and for all his trying Felipe Fats could never catch them, and was cursing roundly in Spanish.

He opened his eyes.

The shadows were getting long under the shade trees. The wind had shifted, coming cool now, down from the mountains. Where the devil was Felipe?

After some consideration, Clint remembered Felipe's strong love of tequila. Could Felipe have spent his eating money on firewater? Maybe he was sitting in some crummy Mexican-style saloon full of smoke and chili with a jug of tequila or pulque or whatever.

Clint couldn't imagine what else could have happened to Felipe. Though it did seem different to believe that a man who'd been this long without food would buy drink. Particularly since Felipe hadn't shown any of the usual signs of a drunk deprived of his bottle during the days of hardship. But maybe a Mexican was different.

Clint went wandering around town keeping his eyes peeled. He saw a fair number of Mexicans, but not Felipe. After a couple of hours of searching, Clint got worried. Now he was wondering if Felipe had deserted.

He went to the livery, half expecting the burros to be gone, but they were still there, perking their ears at him when he came in. Clint went back into the street at a loss as to what to do, and was still thinking about it when from around a corner came Felipe, eyes roaming around, apparently looking for him.

'Where the hell were you, Fats?' Clint demanded.

'Have patience, Cleent. I have been trying to find the Señor Blake Dixon. He is the man you wish to see, no?'

'Did you find him?' Clint had been so

64

concerned with finding Felipe he hadn't been thinking about looking for Dixon. Now the cold determination to take it out on Dixon was returning.

'Sí! He is in the mountains. It is not far. Un jornado only. A day's ride.'

'Well, let's go then. I'll buy some horses. You buy a couple days' grub. But not all chili, maize and tequila.'

'Sí, Cleent, I will do this,' Felipe agreed, taking the money Clint handed him.

They rode out not more than three hours before dusk, but Clint was determined to get there just as soon as they could. He felt himself again now, with a real horse under him, and saddle, and hot on Dixon's trail. All the business of putting up with Felipe and the Indians and the burros had been worth it after all.

They slept on lush grass under a spreading oak tree and awoke fresh and rested. The trail led up a labyrinth of valleys and gullies under towering walls of rock, lush with greenery. It was relatively cool and comfortable after the desert, and there was always water within a stone's throw.

'What does Dixon do? Mine?'

'Sí, Cleent,' Felipe said. 'He is miner.'

'Just a dirt grubber or does he have a real operation?'

65

'It has been said he is panning for the gold, you know? He comes to town every month to buy supplies.'

'By himself?'

'Oh, sí. He is alone. You wish to have business with him, Cleent?'

'Guess you could call it that.'

'You wish to shoot him, no?'

Clint looked at Felipe. Felipe's eyebrows were raised slightly, and he was grinning.

'Felipe, do you love your wife and children?'

'Adelita and los hijos? They are a great burden and a great joy to me, Cleent.'

'Well, I had a wife. I'd just brought her to my ranch in Colorado. Dixon took her screaming from the house. I followed and found her naked and battered to death in the woods.'

'I understand now why you wish to find the Señor Dixon,' Felipe said. 'It is revenge. I would do the same, Cleent. It would be a duty. I would never rest. I would cut him apart a small piece at a time, no? It would be very painful for him. He would pay for his sins with great terrible pain.'

Bloodthirsty words, but Clint felt just that way about it himself, even after five years.

It was late afternoon when they came up a long slope through a grove of aspen and entered a thick stand of fir. The branches were so thick that the trail was only dimly lighted.

Like apparitions, sombreroed Mexicans emerged from the thickets and blocked the trail, crossed shoulder belts of ammunition and rifles gleaming dully.

Clint tugged his horse to a stop, hand hovering near his Colt. He was in no mood to tiptoe around a bunch of Mexican thieves. Determination made his good sense and caution take a back seat.

'You got something to say, say it,' he said to them. 'Otherwise, get out of the way.'

Another Mexican stepped into the trail in front of the others. He was dressed all in white, and wore a brace of well-oiled pearl handled revolvers. He had a flamboyant mustache waxed on the ends, and a thin hard face.

'Hola Felipe,' he said. 'This is the Señor Clint Evans?'

'Sí,' Felipe said. 'Watch his gun. He is very fast. And he has the hot head sometimes. He might not be sensible.'

CHAPTER EIGHT

Clint swung on Felipe. 'You mean to tell me I've rode burros and killed Indians and gone thirsty and hungry all so you could ambush me? What the hell's the point you double-crossing fat tortilla?'

'Cleent, do not be upset. Have patience.' Felipe spread his hands. To the white-suited Mexican he said, 'The señor Cleent Evans has a letter for you.'

'So that's it. Then this is Valenzuela?'

'Sí, señor, I am Garcia Valenzuela. Please, do not be alarmed. I have no wish to harm you. It is merely the letter you have so kindly come all this way to deliver.'

Clint looked from Valenzuela to Felipe and back again, trying to understand what this was really all about. He had the strong feeling that there was something missing. Something was wrong with this, but he couldn't quite figure out what it was just now.

'The letter, señor?' Valenzuela asked pleasantly, flashing white teeth, but Clint also noticed the flinty hardness of Valenzuela's eyes.

Clint debated, then decided under the circumstances, he could part with the letter.

Perhaps, if he watched and listened carefully, he might learn something more about Dixon. Evidently Dixon wasn't here, but perhaps Valenzuela would know where to find him. Perhaps the letter would even make him angry enough to give aid in Dixon's destruction.

Clint handed over the letter. 'Maybe Felipe here has told you. I'm looking for Dixon.'

Valenzuela didn't respond. He read the letter, face completely unreadable. Then he pocketed it.

Then he smiled not quite warmly at Clint and said, 'Please, Señor Evans, you are welcome. Stay as long as you wish. I have good wine and there are many pretty women to dance with.'

Clint knew that there was no way he was going to find out anything if he just rode off. He might be letting himself in for something staying around, but if Valenzuela didn't plan to let him go for some reason, he had plenty of power to carry out his desire in any case.

'Sure, why not,' Clint said to Valenzuela expansively. 'Perhaps we can talk about Dixon.'

Valenzuela didn't acknowledge the last suggestion, but he bowed and begged them to follow him. Horses were led out of the thickets, beautiful animals, worth a lot of money, Clint guessed. Valenzuela's banditry was paying off handsomely, it appeared.

Three hundred yards on along the trail, Valenzuela swung off on a narrow side track which soon led into a narrow high-walled cut in a massive cliff. The horses' hooves kicked loose rocks and the sound echoed eerily with a sort of ringing sound. The cut was about a hundred yards long, and then it opened out into a bowl-shaped area walled solidly with rock and containing an impressive stone building that had a fortress look about it, mostly on account of the long low length of it with small high windows.

They had passed guards, well armed, at the entrance to the cut, and now passed more guards at the point where it opened into the bowl. Clint guessed that these were not all the guards, but that the tops of the cliffs between which the cut went were fairly alive with gun-toting Mexicans. Clint was heartily glad he had not accepted the job of trying to rescue Griego's daughter from here. It would have been a lot more fight than he wanted.

Valenzuela led the way to a large archway in the middle of the building's front wall and dismounted. On a sharp command from him, men came to take the reins of all the riders' horses.

'Come, señores,' Valenzuela said, 'your horses will be taken care of.'

70

Clint, with Felipe at his heels, went through the arch. The inside of the building was done in typical Spanish style, with a zaguán through which one went into the portico, passing through an iron grillwork gate. The portico went around all four sides of the patio, separated from the patio by the row of stone posts supporting arches. The patio was filled with flowers and cages of birds that sang. There was the heavy smell of jasmine flowing around. Several women were sitting on the ledge of the central stone fountain, which was not running. Perhaps it was only for looks and not used anyway.

Clint and Felipe were shown to rooms on the far side of the patio. These rooms, like all the others, had their doors on the portico. The rooms were side by side, and Clint noticed armed guards followed them into the patio and sat down with the women on the fountain ledge.

'I should be much in your debt if you would leave your guns with Pablo,' Valenzuela said politely, as an old man came up. 'He will take very good care of them.'

'I never let my guns out of my reach,' Clint said flatly.

Valenzuela bowed, hands behind his back. 'A very commendable attitude, Señor Evans, especially in this country. But you are quite

71

safe here. I give you my word, señor. Nothing will harm you while you are here. You have seen for yourself how difficult it would be to attack this place, and I have many excellent men. Please, your gun, señor. It is the rule of the house. It frightens the women.'

'I give you my word I will not frighten the women,' Clint said dryly. 'But if you want my gun, you'll have to kill me to get it.'

Valenzuela gesticulated with his thin ring-flashing hands. 'Please, señor, let us not have bad feelings! There is no need, señor. You have done me a great favor in bringing this letter. Am I not grateful? You will have no need of your gun while you are here. Have I not given my word that you are safe?'

Clint headed for the iron grillwork door leading out of the portico.

'You wish to leave, señor?'

'That's what I plan on,' Clint said. He figured it was time to see just how the ground lay. He kept walking.

'I am sorry, señor,' Valenzuela said. 'I was looking forward to intelligent conversation and the sharing of a bottle of wine. But if you must go, then goodby, señor. May God go with you.'

Clint was given his horse and once again bid goodby with seemingly genuine sorrow. Clint rode out, half expecting to be ambushed at any minute, but he rode for two miles without seeing anyone or hearing anyone.

He stopped, swung his horse around and studied his back trail, scratching his chin thoughtfully.

It was plain that he was fresh out of leads without Felipe or any information Valenzuela might give him. All he could do would be cross the Mescalero country again and then hunt some job to keep him going. Perhaps it really was true that Valenzuela meant no harm to him—after all, why should he? If taking the risk of giving up his weapons meant a shot at a lead to Dixon, then it was worth it. After all, one pistol or even a Winchester didn't stand much chance against a whole armed camp.

Clint set his spurs and rode back toward the stronghold. He hadn't gone but a few hundred yards when out of the deepening dusk rode a sombrero on horseback.

Clint was startled into going for his gun. But it was only Felipe.

'Fats, I'm surprised at you. Not going to take advantage of all that tequila and all those pretty women?'

'Señor, I could not let you go. I wish to make explanations, and to tell you that Valenzuela will not harm you. As you have seen, you may leave at any time. He wished only to offer his hospitality.'

'I'm going back. But I want you to tell me straight: do you know where Dixon is?'

'Sí. But it was my duty to bring the letter here.'

'Yeah, I know. Cousins. I'll tell you what I think, Felipe Fats. I think you knew the letter would be worth money to Valenzuela, and since you know I wouldn't just hand it over to you, you led me a wild goose chase up here so that Valenzuela could take it away from me. I don't think you have any more notion where Dixon is than I do.'

'Señor Cleent,' Felipe protested in an aggrieved voice. 'You do me much wrong. I have misled you in a small way, it is true. For this I am very sorry. The letter Pedro gave his word to deliver. Pedro is my cousin, and Señor Valenzuela también. It is for me to deliver this letter. You are right that I fooled you in a small way, but...'

'Small way? Listen, Fats, we nearly got killed. On the way back, those Mescaleros could get us yet.'

'But Señor Cleent, I will take you to Señor Dixon. You must have patience. We should have trust in each other, Cleent. I will not forget that you saved my life.'

Clint could see no point in arguing, and so shut up. They rode on, and with no trouble at all passed all the guards and reentered the

74

natural fortress where Valenzuela had his stronghold.

CHAPTER NINE

Valenzuela treated them to quite a party. The tequila flowed freely, the four guitarists and the three singers raised a powerful river of music, and the girls seemed to dance faster and faster and look prettier and prettier. Clint did not recall the last time he'd had a high old time. Not since well before marrying Margaret.

He had not planned to drink much, in order to keep his wits sharp. But there was no getting Valenzuela to talk about Dixon. Every time Clint brought up the name, Valenzuela acted as though he hadn't even heard. He was polite and seemed anxious that Clint had a good time. Finally, after one or two heady sips of tequila, and a dance with a beautiful señorita, he gave up and enjoyed the party.

The party seemed to go faster and faster until it was just a pleasant heady whirl. Clint danced with nearly every girl there, only vaguely wondering if one of them might be Pepita Griego. At some point the party spun away into nothing.

*　　　*　　　*

He woke up looking at a high white ceiling. For a moment, everything seemed very fine and peaceful. He did not quite recall where he was or what he had been doing recently. He remembered burros like a bad dream and inwardly smiled. Then he thought of Felipe wanting to skin them and actually did smile . . .

And that was his last pleasant thought of the morning. The slight effort required to move his face muscles set off a chain reaction like touching off dynamite inside his head. He groaned, now clearly recalling the tequila and the beautiful señoritas and the guitar music and the sad Mexican songs. He tried to sit up and his head exploded over and over again, with every heartbeat. He tried to keep it down by holding his head in his hands, but the remedy wasn't particularly effective.

After sitting for some minutes to allow the pain to subside, he made a very careful attempt to stand up. This set off more fireworks and he wished he'd had the sense not to let the party get the better of him.

It took him twenty minutes to get dressed. Then he stepped out into the portico and winced at the brightness of the noonday sun

76

on the stone floor of the patio.

'Ah, Señor Evans!' Valenzuela said warmly, coming briskly from somewhere, dressed immaculately as always, smiling. 'You have had a good rest, I trust?'

'You have to shout at me?'

'Ah! The tequila! Hoho, señor, you will have to watch out now. The señoritas are all talking about you!'

'That a fact?' Clint mumbled, holding his head and blinking at the fierce glare of the sun. Funny how it seemed twice as bad here as in the desert.

'Sí señor, it is a fact. You have made quite a reputation among the señoritas. You can dance very well.'

This was blatant flattery. Clint knew he couldn't dance much better than a hog could, but he let it pass. If it pleased this little potentate of a bandit to flatter him, then that was his privilege. Clint was likewise doubtful that the señoritas were much interested in him either, but then you never could tell with señoritas, and he wasn't sure he remembered everything about last night. For instance, he didn't recall undressing and going to bed.

'Looky, Mr. Valenzuela,' Clint said. 'You keep ignoring it when I ask you about Blake Dixon. You seem to know the man, and I am trying to find him. I'm going to ask you once

77

more: would you care to tell me what you know about him?'

Valenzuela eyed him, still smiling, speculatively. 'Señor, I would be honored if you would eat alumerzo with me. Perhaps we can have this discussion you wish so much. I am going to eat now. Come if you are hungry.'

Clint was in too much pain to be hungry, even after eating very little the previous night. He suspected the food would not be very edible, but if Valenzuela was going to flap his jaw about Dixon, Clint wasn't going to pass it up.

The table was massive, carved intricately of some dark and well oiled wood. A lace tablecloth lay over it delicate as a spider web, probably silk by the look of it. Two places were set, but Valenzuela had the fat old lady who was getting ready to serve them set another.

A moment later, a strikingly beautiful dark-skinned girl came into the solemn, high-ceilinged room with a disdainful look on her face.

Valenzuela hastened to hold the chair for her. She swept her skirts up and sat down light as a butterfly on a flower.

'Buenos Días, Señorita,' Clint said, and she acknowledged with a nod.

In Spanish, Valenzuela told her that Señor

78

Evans was a very good friend and a fine dancer, that he had made many señoritas very happy the night before. Again, she nodded, not smiling, acting as though infinitely superior to Valenzuela and the whole of Valenzuela's operation, and to Clint, whoever of whatever *he* might be.

'This is Señorita Pepita Griego,' Valenzuela said. 'She is also visiting us for a short while.'

Clint nodded, not letting on to know more than what he was told.

Lunch, as Clint had feared, was very spicy and almost impossible to eat. However, he made a valiant try, as he talked to Valenzuela about Blake Dixon.

'Who is he?' Clint asked.

'Señor Dixon is a friend of mine. Is he one of your friends also?'

'I know him, at least I know about him.'

'And you are attempting to find him, is this correct?'

'Now you get the idea.'

'It is a fine thing we have a mutual friend. It is a way of becoming better friends ourselves, is it not?'

'I guess if you say so.'

'Would you like more coffee, señor?'

'No thanks. You were about to tell me where I can find Dixon?'

'Ah. He is the hard man to find, no?'

79

Valenzuela's hard black eyes glimmered. 'He communicates with me upon occasion, but I could not tell you exactly where he is, señor. He does not stay long in one place. When I wish to contact him, I send someone to find him. Sometimes it takes a long time.'

'Just what is your connection to this hombre anyhow?'

Something moved in the depths of Valenzuela's eyes as he said, 'We sometimes have business. But we are amigos primarily.'

Clint tried once or twice more to pry out information, but Valenzuela with unfailing politeness and talk slick as calves' slobbers neatly sidestepped the questions.

Pepita Griego, meanwhile, had simply sat there, refusing to eat. Now having studied her more carefully, he noticed the pallor and the way her clothes seemed to hang loosely on her. Her eyes were slightly sunken and her cheeks pinched. She was evidently starving herself. She seemed to have enormous disdain for Valenzuela and no interest in the visitor.

Now Valenzuela turned to her. He pulled a rolled sheet of paper from somewhere and spread it out on the table in front of her and laid a quill pen and bottle of ink at her hand. The paper was blank.

'Are you ready to write to your father?' he asked her pleasantly. 'The messenger can be sent immediately.'

She stared across the ornate room without showing any sign he existed.

'I do not wish to have to impress upon your mind the need for this letter,' he said. 'It will be so much more pleasant if you will be reasonable.'

She ignored him.

He snapped his fingers sharply, and a man, heavily armed, appeared from somewhere.

'Prepare the captive,' Valenzuela ordered in clipped Spanish. Then to Pepita he said, 'You will come with me, please.' He got up and held her chair. He looked at Clint. 'This might perhaps be of interest to you, señor.'

They went into the patio, and then out through the iron grillwork and left the building. There was a stout post driven into the ground near the wall of rock that surrounded them. From a small stone building separate from the main house-fortress, a man with his hands bound behind him was being led towards the post. He was a Mexican, but beyond that Clint could tell nothing. The man was bound back-to the stake and the two men who'd done it stepped of a few paces and began checking the actions of their guns.

'This man,' Valenzuela said to Pepita, 'do you know him?'

Pepita stopped several feet away from the man at the stake and stood proudly, but her face wanted to contort into protest.

'Pepita,' the man at the stake said calmly in Spanish, 'don't do it.'

'He is not by chance your brother Miguel?' Valenzuela asked.

'Miguel . . .' Pepita began. 'I cannot let you die.'

'It is better that I die than the honor of our family die,' Miguel returned firmly.

'It is possible,' Valenzuela suggested, 'that Miguel will not have to die. In five minutes he could be on his way to your father with your letter.'

'Do not do it,' Miguel said flatly. 'I could not return in disgrace. I would not deliver such a letter, Pepita.'

'Miguel,' she said, and tears glistened in her eyes. Clint wondered what the hell this was supposed to have to do with him.

'Don't do it, Pepita,' Miguel said.

'I will,' she said, breaking down. 'I will not let you die.'

'I tell you, Pepita, I will not deliver the letter. It would be dishonorable.'

'Miguel . . .' She put her face in her hands. Clint felt for her, but realized that not knowing what it was all about, it was an emotion to be suspicious of. It was hard to tell

82

who was deserving of what. The thing he wanted was to get shut of these Mexicans and their feud and go hunt for Dixon.

Valenzuela had provided a small writing table and paper and pen, right there in the open, and Pepita sat down tearfully and began writing hurriedly in Spanish. Clint couldn't make it out from where he stood, and didn't know if he might upset Valenzuela and be next at the post if he tried to move around so he could read it. He figured useless curiosity wasn't enough reason to make any moves he wasn't sure of around here.

When she finished, Valenzuela picked up the paper and read it over, smiling, and then carefully rolled it up and sealed it.

Then he said to the guards, 'Shoot him,' and without hesitation they did.

CHAPTER TEN

Pepita, kicking, screaming and struggling, was carried off to the house. Clint had a sour taste in his mouth. Against his better judgement he was thinking about the money he'd taken from Felipe, who'd taken it from Griego's man, and he was thinking maybe he'd like to earn it after all.

He was still toying with the notion, knowing it was plain foolhardy but still having a powerful strong urge to see Valenzuela in his grave, when his hand automatically went to his pocket to check for the money—and found it wasn't there.

'Señor Evans,' Valenzuela was saying smoothly, dabbing at sweat with a silk handerchief. 'It is very unfortunate what happens to the friends of Griego, is it not?'

'Not much of a sport, are you?' Clint remarked, returning Valenzuela's cold hard gaze.

'It is an example of what may happen to those who may desire to oppose me,' Valenzuela said.

'I get your drift, Valenzuela,' Clint said dryly. 'You're warning me off. You'd have done better to do nothing, as far as I am concerned. I don't cotton to threats much. I never had any notion of working for Griego when I found out what he wanted me to do. I've got only one interest, and that's to find Blake Dixon and see he pays for what he did to my wife. I don't want anything to do with any feud you have got going with Griego, or anything else. But killing men that way is the way yellowbellies do it. You wanted to impress me, you'd have fought the man a fair fight.'

Valenzuela smiled. 'You are a fine man, Señor Evans. I am very sorry for this little scene. You must forgive me. I did not know of what material you were made. As for Miguel, it was necessary to kill him. It is a thing you know little about. Do not worry, señor, when I have a man to fight, for whom I have respect, I always fight honorably. But dogs and those who are no better than dogs do not deserve such respect.'

Clint decided he'd better change the subject, or he'd lose his temper.

'Where's Felipe?' he asked.

'I expect he will be up by now. He had much tequila last night!'

Clint went into the house and found Felipe in his room. Clint went in and closed the door.

'Where is it?' Clint demanded.

'Where is what, señor?' Felipe was just getting out of bed, bleary-eyed and evidently with the same kind of headache Clint had had on getting up. Clint's headache was returning.

'The money. Now I know why you wanted me to come back. For the party. And that's another reason you brought me here in the first place. Now where is it?' Clint began searching the pockets of Felipe's pants, which were slung over a chair, he found nothing.

'Señor,' Felipe said softly, holding his head in his hands. 'Oh, señor, do not shout. My

85

head it is the fireworks.'

Clint was in a bad mood. He leaned over and said loudly into Felipe's ear, 'Where did you put it?'

Felipe moaned and fell sideways onto the bedclothes, pulling the pillow over his head.

Clint yanked the pillow away and shook Felipe hard. 'Come on, Fats, show me where you put it. I've about had it with you and your damned cousins and your ways.'

Felipe looked sorrowfully up at Clint. 'Cleent, I do not have it. Why should I steal your money when you have saved my life? It would be so ungrateful. I am a very grateful man, Cleent. I would not do this to you.'

'Well, somebody took it. Either you or one of your cousins. You get it. I want it.'

'But Cleent, Señor Valenzuela would not steal from you. He has much already.'

'The way I hear tell, he has it because he stole it.' The more Clint thought about it, the more he realized the possibility of Valenzuela or one of his men having taken it. It could even have been one of the señoritas he had danced with. How could he ever expect to get it back? He couldn't, unless he could find it in Felipe's possession.

He began searching again. But as far as he could tell, it wasn't in the room. Felipe might have stashed it somewhere else, knowing Clint would suspect him and come looking. But if that was the case, it made searching for it a futile thing. The only thing to do would be wait until Felipe left the stronghold, and then tackle him.

'You plan on hanging your hat here long?' Clint asked.

'But it is up to you, señor.'

'Then we're leaving now. You're going to take me to Dixon. This time, no more doing favors for cousins along the way, got that?'

'Oh, sí, ?Cleent. There is nothing more.'

Clint was relieved to leave the bandit's stronghold behind. For some distance he and Felipe didn't talk at all. Clint figured he'd wait until they were a good long way from Felipe's cousin or whatever Valenzuela was to Felipe before he tried to find out what Felipe had on him. It wasn't that Clint figured he had any more right to the money than Felipe had, but that he figured he had no less right to it. If Griego hadn't been a Mexican in the middle of a feud, Clint would almost certainly have returned the money to him. But under the circumstances, it seemed a good bet that Dixon was in Valenzuela's camp somehow, in spite of the nasty letter, and Clint would have earned whatever money it cost to get rid of him, and if there was money left he could return that and call it even.

This was how Clint rationalized it anyway.

They pulled into Oak Creek towards sundown.

'Well,' Clint said. 'I haven't got a cent. You want to eat, or sleep someplace besides on the ground, you better fish out that clink of coin you took off me.'

'Cleent, I have told you, I have nothing. But we do not have to go hungry.'

'Oh no?'

'Oh no, señor Cleent. You can shoot, no?'

'You plan to hold up somebody?'

'Oh no, Cleent!'

'Say, didn't you get paid for delivering that letter?'

'No,' Felipe said sadly, 'I have nothing, señor. But listen. Can you act drunk?'

Clint, suddenly realizing what Felipe might have in mind, grinned. 'You are an ingenious fellow, Felipe Fats.'

Ten minutes later, Clint, having found a few empty whiskey bottles and piled them in a haphazard group next to an alley wall, sat down amongst them, loosened his shirt and crumpled his hat. Then he waited.

It was not a long wait. He presently heard Felipe's voice raised in an argument with somebody, bragging. 'My partner, he can shoot the legs off a fly blindfolded. You will see. He is much better than you. You will see.'

'You been drinkin' too much tequila,' an amused voice said calmly. 'Where'd you say your pard was? Fetch him out, vaquero. I'm tired a hearin' you talk.'

'You wait, señor. Wait right here. I will find him. He is probably at the livery. I will find him, and then we will see.'

By the sound of the voices, it appeared that there were people gathering, waiting to see if there was going to be something to watch. Clint got up and, with a whiskey bottle in one hand, staggered out of the alley and drunkenly looked one way, then the other, let out a slobbery giggle and sat down against the cornerpost of the building nearest him as though to watch.

Felipe was waddling quickly down the street, looking all around. He went all the way to the far end of town, and Clint figured Felipe was leaving him plenty of acting room, so he made use of it.

'Hey, friend,' he called to the nearest of the crowd that was gathering. 'Wathsh goin' on?'

'Goin' to be a shootin' contest,' the man said. 'Some Mexican thinks his partner can shoot real good. Wants to put him up against Barnham here.'

'Hooss Barrum?'

'You ain't never heard tell of Blur Barnham? Well, he's just about the most fine

89

gun handler in these parts. . .'

But the fellow's friend, a little quick-eyed short fellow, nudged him and said, almost too soft for Clint to make out, 'Shut up, Jake. Suppose he wants to put down some money?'

'Course,' the fellow went on talking, loudly, 'we don't know who this Mexican's friend is. Maybe he's the best in the county, or the whole state. Care to put money on somebody?'

'I can shoot . . . maybe you want to put money on me?'

The two men and the others standing around thought that was pretty funny, and got a good big laugh out of it. Clint saw Felipe coming back along the street and decided it was time for him to get off the scene.

He went along the alley band then behind a few buildings and then, acting a little unsteady on his feet, but just in control, wandered out into the street not twenty paces in front of Felipe.

'Oh, Cleent, I have been looking for you,' Felipe said in a loud voice. 'There is a man who believes he can shoot better than you. But I tell him and the others that it is not true. I tell them that there is nobody faster than you. I tell him you can shoot the legs off the fly for twenty paces.'

Clint, with exaggerated sobriety, turned to look at the group of people. He said, 'Hoos thish man?'

Felipe led the way along to the group of men. They were jostling each other and smiles were everywhere.

'Who says that Barnham can shoot better than Cleent?' Felipe demanded. 'Put your money down!'

There was a lively session while bets were placed. There was a lot of talk and many grinning faces. Clint was amazed at the amount of money that piled up on Barnham. Felipe reached into his pocket and a look of horror crossed his face.

He turned to Clint. 'Cleent, you have the money to cover these bets?'

Clint barked out a loud laugh, and then was quiet.

'Señores,' Felipe said earnestly. 'I have burros. Three burros. They are very fine animals. I also have two horses, with fine saddles. They are also very good animals. I will put them against the money you have betted. Is this acceptable, señores? These animals, they are worth much money.'

The men consulted with each other. Then they wanted to see the animals. Felipe led the way to the livery, where the burros were still being looked after, their keep having been paid in advance through one more night. The horses were tied up to the public rail in front of the nearest saloon. Those that had bet against Felipe finally agreed among themselves that the horses and burros would do, and everybody proceeded to the town limits on foot, since it was not far. Clint walked with great care, making a project out of stepping over horse dung in the street. There was much surreptitious winking and nudging amongst the men over this.

The man Clint was to shoot against, known as Blur Barnham for the way his hand was reputed to move when going for his gun—so Clint had heard—was a tall, lanky fellow with a flowing mane of hair and a calm smile. He worried Clint more than a man with flashy guns and polished boots might have. It seemed likely that this Barnham might be damned good with his Colt.

The group halted under some big oak trees that overspread the trail south of town. The sun was getting mighty low in the west now, throwing long shadows.

'Well, Mr. Evans,' Barnham said politely, 'what kind of shootin' you go in for? I think I saw a fly land on that tree down there, but I ain't sure.'

Clint laughed wildly, and stepped sideways a couple of steps as though to catch his balance.

'Somebody draw a bull's-eye on that tree,'

someone directed, indicating an oak thirty yards away. 'Don't make it too big.'

A man went down there and with his knife cut out a small piece of bark. Then he came back. 'See it?' he asked.

'Go ahead,' Barnham invited.

'No, señor, you go ahead,' Clint said, bowing low, and making everybody laugh.

Felipe was a consummate actor. He began to step back and forth from one leg to the other, as though having second thoughts. He kept watching Clint out of the corner of his eye. This helped keep the smiles on the men's faces.

Barnham drew very slowly and deliberately and fired.

'Go ahead, Evans,' one of the crowd said.

'Oh no,' Clint said. 'Somebody see if the bullet hit the tree. If it's in the bull's-eye, I'll drop mine on top and you'll never ... you'll tell ... you'll *never* tell if there's one or two bullets in it!'

A general guffaw went through the group, but one man did trot down to see. He came back with the news that the bullet was dead center the bull's-eye.

Clint squinted hard at the tree, leaning forward slightly and squeezing up his eyes as though staring into the desert sun. Then he pulled out his pistol, managing to do it awkwardly, and held it out with both hands and sighted carefully, still squinting fiercely. He made sure he was aiming it at the wrong tree.

Men nudged each other. Clint took a deep breath, closed his eyes and turned his head away.

Then he staggered and lost his aim. He caught his balance and then went through the whole performance again, this time at another tree, still not the one the target was on. Again he got to the point of shooting and while everyone involuntarily held his breath he staggered and lost his aim.

Now, wondering inwardly if he was overdoing it, he glanced around at the faces, but saw only suppressed laughter and turned back to survey the trees, pistol dangling loosely in one hand.

'Felipe,' he said in a heavy stage whisper.

Felipe stepped closer.

'Which tree is it, Felipe?' he asked in the stage whisper.

'Oh, señor,' Felipe moaned. 'It is that one.' And he pointed, partially hiding the pointing from the crowd.

Clint raised the pistol again, this time without apparently aiming at all, and fired.

When they went to examine the tree, they still saw only the one hole, and they began demanding the horses and burros, talking about who would be the best men to sell them to in order to get the highest price.

'Señores,' Felipe protested. 'Please, señores, dig in thee hole, señores.'

After a certain amount of debate, it was done, and everybody went silent for a moment when two bullets were found in the hole, one on top of the other.

Then there were whistles and ejaculations of surprise. Then calls for another round. Clint meanwhile stowed his gun with an elaborate flourish and peered down his nose at Blur Barnham.

'Howshat fer shootin', Blue Barroom?'

'The name is Blur Barnham,' Barnham said with just a slight edge of annoyance in his tone. Over the general hubbub he demanded, 'Anybody got something to throw?'

'We can throw rocks,' somebody in the crowd suggested. 'Unless they're too small to hit,' he added, baiting them.

'If I can see it, I can hit it,' Barnham said curtly. 'Toss away.'

'Ready then?' the man asked, and when he threw up a fist-sized rock, Barnham drew and shattered it with a bullet.

'Your turn, Evans,' the thrower said, and everybody jostled for a view and held their breaths again.

The rock went up, then started down, while Clint just looked at it as though fascinated. It was four or five feet from the ground before he drew. The rock exploded into fragments. There was a collective sigh of amazement and disappointment.

'Two rocks,' Barnham said tersely. He was a competitive type, that was plain. The rocks were thrown and he got them both. Then two more were thrown, and Clint staggered around until they were a few feet off the ground, then shattered them both.

'Three rocks,' Barnham said. He got them, but had to use four bullets to do it. All eyes turned to Clint. There was no nudging and jostling now.

Clint got his three with just three bullets, and then drilled the other three bullets into the largest of the fragments before they hit the ground. Then he doubled over with apparently drunken laughter.

CHAPTER ELEVEN

After liverying their horses, Clint and Felipe got a couple of rooms in the best hotel in town. Then they ate meals in separate restaurants and returned to Clint's room.

Splitting the take in half, they wound up with something over fifty dollars apiece.

'Cleent, that was the most funny thing,' Felipe said, as he had said several times now. 'It is still much in my mind how they looked when we took their money! They just could not believe it!'

'Worked like a charm,' Clint admitted. 'I was worried. I thought sure Barnham was better than he turned out to be. He had the look of it. I guess we were lucky.' He paused. 'Looky, Felipe, where do we go now, hunting Dixon?'

Felipe rubbed his chubby hands together. 'Señor, I have said that Dixon is in this town. But I do not think he is after all. But do not fear, there are people I can ask. We will find the Señor Dixon, Cleent, do not fear. But I will not know where to look until I ask certain friends.'

Clint nodded, wondering whether to believe Felipe or not. He decided that for now, there was nothing better to do but see what Felipe would turn up.

'Cleent, we have money. I am very thirsty. I think I will look for some fun.'

'After last night? That wasn't enough for you?'

'That was last night. This is today, señor.'

Felipe went out. Clint decided not to try to

97

stop him. It would not fit in well with his plans. When he was sure that Felipe was out of the hotel, he went along to Felipe's room and jiggered the door lock with his knife. For about an hour he searched the room, but at last he gave it up. The money was just not there.

He decided that he would wait until Felipe returned drunk, and then he would check his clothes. It was as important to find out if Felipe was telling the truth about not having the money as it was to get the money itself. The fifty some odd dollars he had left of the money he'd made today took the edge off the need to get the money away from Felipe. In fact, the more he thought about it, the more he suspected Felipe was telling the truth and it had been one of the señoritas who had stolen the money.

Clint had not quarreled with Felipe's assertion that he had not been paid anything by Valenzuela, thinking to locate the evidence to refute that later, and maybe corner Felipe into talking more about Dixon. But now, thinking about it, it seemed hard to believe that Felipe would not have at least bought meals and livery for them if he had any money. He could always explain that the money had come from Valenzuela, even if it hadn't. Even Felipe wasn't that much of a hoarder of money.

But the main reason he was inclined to believe Felipe was that he thought of him as a friend. They had been through a lot together. Even the misleading Felipe had done didn't seem too bad in retrospect. After all, Felipe was related to Valenzuela, lowdown scoundrel that the bandit was, and Clint kept thinking about Felipe's family living in the brush hut. Could you blame the man for getting money anywhere he could? Valenzuela, at least sometimes, paid him for his help, and what man in Felipe's position would pass it up? Clint also thought of how he himself had treated Felipe from the beginning. It had been an invitation to Felipe to lie and steal.

Smiling still at the smoothness with which he and Felipe had won money today, Clint was feeling so mellow and friendly towards Felipe that he began to think Felipe probably deserved the money he'd taken from Griego's man more than he, Clint, did. Clint decided he might not take the money from Felipe, even if he found it on him. And then he began to wonder what business it was of his to go searching Felipe's room and his clothes, and after a short while, Clint got into bed and went to sleep, dreaming peacefully of pretty señoritas dancing. The burros were finally gone from his dreams.

He woke up, however, in a very different mood, thinking about Miguel being shot. He could still mentally hear the shots being fired, see Miguel jerking three times before slumping against the rope bindings. The image mingled with the image of his wife lying dead and battered in the woods, and though it was not yet light, he couldn't get back to sleep.

He got out of bed and went for a walk along the mostly empty quiet Main Street of Oak Creek. The rumble of ore pouring out of the mines continued, and there were still the cries of a few teamsters and creak of a few ore wagons, but that was about all. The air was still, cool, and the trees hulked over the town against a barely lightening sky full of stars that seemed to have lost the mystery of night.

For something to do, Clint went along to the livery to look in on the horses and burros. He lit a lantern hanging on a hook inside the door and walked into the main floor of the barn.

'What the . . .' he began, then stopped.

The horses and burros were gone.

'The thieving, conniving Mexican tortilla chili pepper bean head,' Clint muttered, double-checking to make sure the animals hadn't simply been moved to different stalls— they hadn't.

Even took *my* horse, Clint brooded. Hadn't the common decency to leave a man his horse. That called for hanging, by the law. It would be too good for the chili pepper.

Clint roused out the livery man, who was not pleased by the disturbing of his sleep. He was a short, wiry little man with cynical eyes. He rolled off his corn-shuck tick and demanded what the hell Clint wanted.

'I want a horse, a fast horse, and a saddle.'

'Rent or buy?'

'Buy ... no, rent,' he changed his mind, remembering the shortness of his funds. A good horse would likely cost more than fifty dollars, even without a saddle. And he would need supplies for a couple of days at least.

The livery man drove a hard bargain and Clint had to part with all but two dollars of his money to get the horse and saddle and two days supply of beans and sourdough.. Clint couldn't wait for the business section of town to open up to buy food, so paid dearly for stocks from the liveryman's own larder.

'I want that horse back in four days,' the liveryman reminded him sharply from the doorway. 'One day longer, and I send the sheriff after you for horse thievin'.'

107

Clint rode south out of town hell-for-leather. It was his guess Felipe had left town just as soon as he left the hotel saying he was going drinking. That gave him eight or nine hours head start. Clint had no way of knowing for sure which way Felipe had gone, but he doubted Felipe would have more business at Valenzuela's, and it seemed likely that he figured he had a pretty good haul for one trip and was heading home. So, Clint set out into the desert going south, pushing the horse along at a good clip, aware that once the sun came up and the heat began to shimmer in the desert, the horse wouldn't be able to keep it up.

Clint knew this was a desperate kind of gamble. He had bought two days of travelling time south to catch up with Felipe. The desert was huge and Felipe knew it well while Clint did not. And then there were the Mescaleros. Of course, it was true that Felipe was vulnerable, having such an array of burros and horses. Yet, Clint had a suspicion that Felipe would manage somehow. He might fear Indians, but he could also fool Indians, if anybody could.

Clint knew that if he got pinned down at any time during the next four days, he would have the sheriff after him and a charge of horse thieving would hang over his head.

With the desert full of Mescaleros, the possibility was not remote. The way Clint preferred to look at it was, if he got pinned down, and was overdue, a posse of armed men would be along to side him against the Indians.

As dawn stretched across the land, Clint began searching the horizon in all directions constantly, watching for both Felipe and Indians. He had seen nothing by noon, and gave the horse a short break to crop a patch of grass and drink some water from his hat. Clint took a sip himself and then swung up and dug in his heels.

The heat of the day was almost enough to make Clint stop for a break, but the knowledge that Felipe might do that made Clint press on. He figured it was his chance to do some catching up.

By nightfall, he had still seen no sign of Felipe, but then he'd seen no sign of Indians either, and so he called it even and halted for a two hour rest. He ate a small amount, about half a meal, and rested, letting the horse crop grass. He decided that with the burros, Felipe stood no chance of moving even half as quickly as a man on a good horse could. So, Clint figured, if he pushed on after the moon came up, for at least a few hours, he ought to be somewhere near as far into the desert as

Felipe, and in the morning there might be something to see.

Clint carried out this plan, and in the morning rode up onto the top of a slight rise to take a long and careful look around the horizon. He had the feeling he was being watched, but it seemed plain that he was alone on this piece of country. Not a sign of burros or horses or Indians or anything but mesquite and cactus as far as he could see across the sand in any direction.

Unfortunately he had no way to tell if he was just paralleling Felipe or had not yet caught up with him—or even had passed him somewhere. Clint debated a while, and then decided he would ride southeast, then southwest in a zigzag motion, stopping on high points to take a look.

By noon, the horse, which he'd run pretty hard for the conditions, was slowing down and losing interest. Clint had still seen nothing. But he kept feeling as though eyes were watching him. The Mescaleros worried him. He was certain they knew he was there. What were they waiting for? Clint took to snapping his head around to look behind him suddenly as he rode on his zigzag course all afternoon. But he never saw anything.

That evening as darkness fell, Clint became irritable. It was plain he had failed. And who could tell what it would cost in excitement and bloodshed to get back to town. And even once he got there, all he could do would be get a job of some kind to make money so he could buy a horse and a pack horse and supplies and plenty of ammunition. Then he would ride south and find Felipe's hut and, he hoped, Felipe. This was going to come out of Felipe's hide.

In the morning, Clint reluctantly started back for Oak Creek. About midway through the morning, Clint brought up short and listened.

After a moment, he shook his head and nudged his horse on. But then he heard it again—definitely shooting.

He rode on cautiously, unwilling to ride into the middle of fight with Indians, if that was what it was. He topped a rise and was startled to see Mescaleros riding in and out of gunsmoke which lay thickly over a mesquite thicket—and from the thicket the unmistakable braying of burros.

There was no reason they *had* to be Felipe's burros, but Clint was sure they were just the same. He had half a mind to just get back down off the rise and wait for the shooting to stop, and the Indians to take what they wanted and leave. And then see if Felipe was the victim, and whether he was dead or alive.

But for some reason Clint didn't do that. Instead, like a fool, he rode down on the doings with his Winchester in hand. He pulled up when within handy range, and slammed the Winchester to his shoulder and began knocking Indians loose of their saddles.

This surprised them considerably, and things got confused among them and they began whirling their horses and riding off in all directions. From the cloud of smoke surrounding the mesquite thicket a rifle snapped at them energetically. Somebody was still very much alive in there.

Now the Indians began to understand what had happened, and in rage they came whooping and yelling up the slight rise at him, firing off volleys of shots. Clint had the advantage of them, since he didn't have to shoot from the back of a galloping horse, and he dropped about half of them before they got two thirds the distance to him.

The other half, perhaps on signal, suddenly whirled and rode off east across the desert in a cloud of dust, the gun in the thicket still scolding them, although they were quickly out of reasonable range.

As the smoke cleared, Clint rode down on the thicket, Winchester on his thigh, barrel aimed at the sky.

'Howdy, Fats,' he said. 'Little brisk this

morning?'

'Oh, señor Cleent! You have saved my life a second time! How can I ever repay you, Señor Cleent, for all you have done for me?'

'You can start by taking your clothes off,' Clint said reasonably, dropping the Winchester so it pointed at Felipe's midsection.

'Señor, I do not understand this thing you ask me to do. Nevertheless it is unnecessary to point the gun at me, Cleent. I will do as you ask without the insult of a threat of a gun.'

'Quit flapping your lip and drop your drawers.'

Felipe looked nervous. But he did as he was asked.

'Now, toss your clothes up here.'

Clint went through them, and found two things which interested him: money, and Pepita's letter to her father. Clint tossed down the clothes.

'Señor,' Felipe begged, 'do not be angry with me. I am only a poor sheepherder. I have a beeg family and no money. Have compassion, señor.'

'You know, last night I was thinking maybe I had been too hard on you. I thought you were basically honest and that it was only a hard life that made you the way you are. But I think you have a hard life because you are crooked and a thief. One day it will get you in big trouble, Fats. Somebody'll put a bullet between your eyes one of these days. You do not know how tempted I am to do that myself, right now. You have caused me no end of trouble. I ought to skin you alive and leave you for the buzzards. I'd do it too, only I want Dixon, and you're my lead. First, we have to take this rented horse back to town. Then we're going to ride to find Dixon. You won't see the last of me until we do find Dixon. Then you can have the letter. I'll keep the money, by way of compensation for all the cussing energy you've cost me. You understand, Fats?'

'Sí, señor Cleent,' Felipe said meekly. 'I have treated you poorly, have I not?'

'You have.'

'I am sorry, Cleent. It is much temptation for a poor man like me. I drink too much sometimes, you know?'

'Is that a fact,' Clint said, not really listening. He already knew how the conversation would go, and it was getting boring to have to have it every other day or so.

'Sí,' Felipe said eagerly. 'Last night I have a drink, you know?' He was getting on his horse. 'I begin to think, you know? I think about this beautiful horse and all the burros, and I think perhaps I need them more than you. I think perhaps you can always make the money, no? You can shoot, you are Americano, you are smart and you are strong. You can do anything, no?'

'Save it,' Clint said.

'But poor Felipe. He is only a poor Mexicano, a sheepherder, a man with nothing, señor. A man who must make his money how he can. A big family too—and you have no family, sí? It is a lot of mouths to feed. I think I can sell the burros in Crooked Creek, and the horses are worth much anywhere, no? Perhaps Adelita will be able to buy a new dress, eh? It is so bad for Adelita to become beautiful with a new dress? Is not this worth a horse and some burros?'

'I don't want to hear about it, Fats.'

'It is only that I try to explain, Señor Cleent, so you will understand. I do not wish to hurt you. But it is the way the world passes, is it not?'

'Shut up, Fats.'

'I think you are a fine, understanding man, Señor Cleent,' Felipe said reverently.

'Yeah,' Clint said, and stuck a toothpick in the corner of his mouth.

CHAPTER TWELVE

They rode back to Oak Creek without further Indian trouble. Clint was careful to bind Felipe hand and foot at night. Clint returned the horse and got the impression that the liveryman had been hoping Clint would be late so he could send the sheriff after him.

'Okay, Fats, where to?' Clint asked, as they settled into the hotel room that night—one room because Clint wasn't about to let Felipe pull the same stunt again.

'Señor, I must be very honest with you. I do not know where Señor Dixon is. I know only that Pedro must have seen him or seen someone who had passed him the letter. But as to where the Señor Dixon is, I do not know.'

'I see. Well, I don't figure it that way. I figure you do know. What's more, I'm not cutting you loose until you find him for me. So if you don't know, then you'd best find out.'

'Señor Cleent, I would like to help you, for I would like to have the burros. I am very poor, as you have seen for yourself. But it might be a long time. My family will worry about me. And then there is the letter to Señor

Griego. It is very important. I must deliver it very soon. Señor Valenzuela has allowed three weeks only for a reply. It will take a long time to get to the hacienda—perhaps two weeks. It will take longer than three weeks for a reply now. Señor Valenzuela will be very angry. He is dangerous when he is angry. Señor, it is my suggestion to deliver the letter and bring Señor Valenzuela his reply first, and *then* we will look for Señor Dixon.'

Clint was in no mood to be put off yet again. On the other hand, having met Valenzuela and suspecting that Felipe was probably telling something like the truth about rapid delivery of the letter, Clint was inclined to go along with Felipe. One thing Clint didn't figure he needed was Valenzuela on his tail. Life was complicated and difficult enough now without that.

'Okay, Fats, we take Griego the letter. We bring back the reply. Maybe we'll run into Dixon along the way somewhere. He's mixed up with Valenzuela somehow.' As an afterthought, Clint asked, 'You don't happen to know just what the connection is between Valenzuela and Dixon, do you?'

Felipe appeared to consider.

'Señor Cleent, you have saved my life now twice. This is worth something, is it not?'

'Well, your life better be worth something,

111

if I keep saving it. It's costing me a lot of trouble to keep you alive.'

'It is worth much to me, señor,' Felipe said seriously. 'I do not think Valenzuela would allow me to live if he finds out I have told you about Dixon. But I will tell you in any case. It is something I can give for my life.'

Clint adjusted the toothpick and lay back against the headboard to listen.

'The Señor Dixon, he is very important to Señor Valenzuela. Señor Valenzuela, he meets the Señor Dixon two years ago, when Señor Dixon comes to him. The Señor Dixon, he has some information, he says, and he will sell it for a part of the profit to be made. At this time, Señor Valenzuela, he is not much better than me. He is only a poor sheepherder, who must take money from gringos to live. He has a small number of friends who help him. They have become known as dangerous, because they have killed three men once, and the gringo sheriff, he is after them. Well, the Señor Dixon, he says he works for the Tracker Detectives, who are to watch that the gold and silver from the mills is not stolen. The gold and silver, it is sent out at certain secret times, and is hidden in certain wagons, because there has been much holding up. The Señor Dixon, he knows when they are sent because he works for those who protect the gold and silver. He says he will sell to Señor Valenzuela the knowledge of when gold or silver is to be sent from town, and in return desires half of the profits.'

'So Dixon's Valenzuela's spotter.'

'Sí. That is how Valenzuela has become rich and has built his stronghold.'

'Dixon must be just as rich then.'

'Sí.'

'Then he must be useless now, since it doesn't figure that he's still working as a guard and just burying his wealth.'

'Oh no, señor, he does not work anymore. But he still has the connections, no? He finds out and then tells Señor Valenzuela.'

'I'd think Valenzuela would get tired of giving him half and get the connections himself.'

'Señor, it would be impossible. It requires trust, and no gringo will trust a Mexicano.'

'Can't imagine why that should be so. How is it that somebody doesn't catch on to Dixon and jail him? If the holdups come off like clockwork, it seems likely that the mining company would either go out of business or change guard companies.'

'Señor Dixon does not give information on Oak Creek only. He can find out about gold being moved in any town in the mountains or two weeks travel in any direction. He has long ears, very long, señor.'

'But you don't know where this wealthy longeared filth lives?'

'It is not something Señor Dixon wishes known.'

'But Valenzuela knows.'

'I am sure.'

'But you don't.'

'No, señor.'

'And his messengers?'

'No, Cleent. I am a messenger, and I do not know. Letters to him can be left at any saloon and they will find the way to Señor Dixon.'

'Well, seems to me the thing to do is follow one of the messages.'

'This would be very difficult, señor. Everyone is afraid of Señor Dixon. He has much power. No one will allow the message to be seen changing hands.'

'Well, Felipe, let's have your wrists.'

'Cleent, I will not run. I swear upon my mother's holy grave. . .'

'The hands, Fats.'

Clint tied Felipe's wrists behind him, and then tied him down to the legs of the heavy dresser. Then Clint rolled his own blanket out on the bed and went to sleep.

Not long after sunup, they were riding southeast out of town along the sluggish creek. Clint, toothpick in teeth, was pondering Mescaleros. All this crossing of Mescalero desert had a way of wearing you down, and making you jumpy.

The burros were not slow to give trouble. At the point where it was time to turn south away from the creek into the desert, the burros decided they'd rather roll in the mud of the creek bottoms. Felipe's advice was to let them do it for a few minutes. Clint, keeping a tight rein on his temper and aware that the nightmares about burros would be sure to return tonight, agreed. It took an hour to coax the burros into the desert and get under way again.

As it turned out, the crossing of the desert wasn't a problem. They saw no Indians, though the concern that Indians might be about to attack at any moment was nearly as bad in itself. The burros were enough to drive anybody but a Mexican crazy, but by the time Felipe's brush hut appeared as a dot on the horizon, Clint had once again grown accustomed to the critters and was grudingly appreciative that they had helped bring him and Felipe safely across the desert.

'How do you navigate across that place, anyway?' Clint asked, struck by the way they were coming out on Felipe's isolated hut with as much accuracy as a train on rails found the town it was headed for. Clint could have found it eventually, but not with this kind of accuracy.

Felipe shrugged. 'It is not difficult. I go where it is I wish to go.'

'Ah, so that explains it.'

Adelita, Felipe's wife, looked at Clint sourly. For that matter, she looked at Felipe sourly and the first thing she did was complain to him that she had been even sicker while he was away, and that the children had caused her much concern and worry. She practically accused him of deserting her. But Felipe beamed. He took it all as though the warmest welcome and embraced his wife and kissed her enthusiastically. Several rattily clothed and dour-faced children looked silently on, and when he hugged them also, took it all impassively.

They stayed there the night. Clint made an effort to eat Adelita's cooking, but it tasted like fried bedbugs in chili sauce and he had trouble keeping it down. He was offered a mat and a tight corner inside the hut to sleep, but the thick air, the coughing and snoring and squabbles between the children, and the elbows and knees which prodded him continuously made him give it up. He went out into the fresh air upwind of the hut and here finally went peacefully to sleep.

He woke up to find a rattler curled up

under the edge of his blanket. With extreme care, he got clear and then shot the rattler, and Adelita cooked it for breakfast, mixing in a few dozen chili peppers and so on. Clint got a little down, and washed out the fire in his throat which burned all the way down, with black coffee, and then Felipe went into a long and apologetic explanation of what he had to do. His wife waved her arms and scolded him furiously for deserting her again, he kept explaining that it was necessary that he do this in order to get money, and that in any case it was for his cousin Valenzuela.

They rode off with Adelita screaming accusations at them and Felipe smiling and waving gaily.

'Is she not wonderful?' he said to Clint.

'She sure can talk.'

'This she can do!' Felipe agreed, beaming as though it was wonderful.

'Looky, Felipe, I've been thinking. I don't know why I didn't do this before, while we were in Oak Creek. I'm going to leave a message for Dixon. Let's ride over to Crooked Creek and find a saloon.'

'We are going that way in any case. But what will you write?'

'I'm going to tell him I want to talk to him.'

'And then you will hope he will allow you to speak with him? And you will shoot him? It is

117

very clever, but very dangerous. He will have men watching. I do not advise this, Cleent.'

'You have a better way?'

'Señor, there is no good way. The Señor Dixon is a very dangerous man. You have something to settle with him, you must settle it.'

'I'm still going to stay with you, Felipe. In case I don't get an answer. When you deliver the reply to Valenzuela, I'm going with you, unless there is a message from Dixon. I'll see that Valenzuela opens up about Dixon.'

'That is not a safe thing, Señor Cleent. Valenzuela will crush you.'

'I know what he's apt to try. But there may be no other way. You've told me he's the only man who knows where Dixon is. If Dixon won't talk to me, I'll have to find him. And the only way to do that is by making Valenzuela open up.'

'I am glad I am not you, Cleent,' Felipe said soberly. 'I am glad it is not my wife who is dead so that I must kill Dixon. It is a dangerous thing. You will not live. You will give up your life because of your dead wife.'

'The hell.'

'But you must do this, I understand. I would do it in your place, Cleent, but I would not like to die.'

They rode into Crooked Creek two hours

after lunchtime, the burros having been frolicsome that morning and one having therefore lost a pack in a mesquite thicket. The straps had to be repaired and it took half an hour.

Crooked Creek was just as full of gunsmoke and excitement as ever. When they rode up the street, three gunfights were going on at once, and a bunch of drunken miners were chasing a playful dog which had somebody's hat in his mouth. It was an amazement to Clint that there was anything left of the town at all after such a continuous barrage of destruction for so long. When a tent was blown down, or burned or run down by rambunctious men, it was always set right up again in hasty fashion, doing only the barest minimum of work required to do the repair. The result was a shabbiness and atmosphere of carelessness that pervaded the whole town, and if the claims all played out and everybody moved away, there would be nothing here but a couple of adobe walls inside a week, and they would crumble soon under the wear of blowing sand and occasional sudden flooding caused by desert downpours.

Clint hunted up a scrap of paper and borrowed a played out quill pen and some ink and wrote a note.

'Mr. Blake Dixon—

'I want to talk to you. It's important for both you and me—life or death. I'll be waiting.

'The name is

Clint Evans'

He folded it, sealed it with wax from a candle, wrote Dixon's name on the outside and walked into the nearest saloon.

'See this gets to Dixon,' he said, handing it to the barkeeper.

The barkeeper eyed him, then the note, which he had quickly dropped below the bar out of sight of the other patrons.

'What's your pleasure?' he asked.

'Whiskey.'

He drank it off, paid for it and left.

'You have done it?' Felipe asked.

'Yep.'

'Señor Cleent, I will tell you now, in case I do not get a chance again before you die. You are a fine man. I have much respect for you, and I will pray for your soul in heaven.'

'Don't deal me out yet, Fats. I'll likely outlive you.'

They rode south for the border.

CHAPTER THIRTEEN

The Griego hacienda was in the foothills of the Sierra Madre not very far over the border into Mexico. It was a sunny, rich spot halfway between the brutal wastes of the desert and the impenetrable jumble mass of the Sierra Madre. The Griego hacienda ran cattle and did it on a grand scale. As he rode with Felipe over a hill and had a view of the sprawl of the buildings near a sparkling river, the mass of the mountains behind and fluffs of distant summer clouds overhead, Clint drew a deep breath. He had always thought of Mexico as desert and endless squalid repetitions of Felipe. But it appeared there was wealth here in places.

They passed a group of vaqueros, looking prosperous and healthy for their kind, whooping a bunch of cows into a bunch to drive off somewhere. Felipe waved and a couple of them waved back.

After a half hour, during which it seemed that the buildings got no closer, they dropped behind a ridge and when they topped it a few minutes later, they were almost in the dooryard.

Felipe was known here, and because Clint

was with Felipe, he was also accepted with friendly politeness. Yet, Clint had the feeling that it was nothing more than politeness, that he was being tolerated, not trusted. Clint didn't care a hang for that, but figured he'd stay next to Felipe. He wasn't confident he wouldn't be ambushed if he was separated from the tortilla chili pepper.

Their animals were taken care of by cordial vaqueros who joked with Felipe about the burros. Then they were shown into the house, which went in for the usual Spanish architecture: high-ceilings, a patio full of flowers and caged birds in the middle. The uniformed man who had let them in took them along to a room that seemed taller than it was long and whose white stucco walls were hung with what looked like priceless paintings and whose furniture was equally valuable. Lying in a huge bed under a canopy of rich silk tapestries was a shrivelled little figure in a white nightcap and bedclothes showing a hunting scene. The man's head was propped up gently by the man who let them in, and Felipe approached the bedside.

'Hola, Felipe,' Griego said weakly, trying to smile. Continuing in Spanish, he said, 'So, my cousin, what is occurring at that scoundrel's camp? Do you have a message for me?'

Clint had passed the letter from Pepita to

Felipe before they entered the house, and now Felipe passed the letter to Griego, who took it in a bony, shaking hand.

'Who is your American friend, Felipe?' he asked, as he fumbled trying to open the seal.

'Señor Smith. He is a fine man who has saved my life twice in the past short while. He is a friend, you need not fear.'

As they had agreed, Felipe did not mention Clint's name to Griego, since they didn't want to be asked to explain the death of Griego's messenger, Antonio.

'Could you open this for me, my hands shake too much. It is from Pepita, Felipe?' The old man's eyes had a yearning in them which made Clint feel the old man's loss and concern.

Felipe got the seal off the letter and opened it, then passed it to Griego.

'Muchas gracias,' Griego said, and struggled glasses onto his nose so that he could read the letter.

For a few moments there was silence while the old man read. Then he threw the sheet down in disgust, becoming animated.

'This is preposterous!' he said in Spanish. 'It is inconceivable. I do not believe this at all. Pepita would never wish to marry that scoundrel. She would never willingly write such a letter.' Then he looked appealingly at

123

Felipe. 'Tell me, Felipe, that it was not her wish to write this letter. She would not have run away purposely to marry this bandit who murders in cold blood! And now she writes a letter saying she wishes to marry him! It is not true, Felipe, is it? Can you tell me?'

Felipe, with his sombrero by the rim with both hands, tapped it against his knees.

'Señor Griego,' he said, 'it is possible that the little I know may be of use.'

'I am aware that you are a poor man,' Griego said when Felipe paused. 'I may be able to help you very much today, if the wind blows right.'

'I would not think of taking money from my own cousin,' Felipe said with a self-deprecating wave of his hand.

'But I insist. Perhaps your Adelita would like some medicine, or perhaps a new dress would cheer her spirits.'

'It is very possible that a new dress would lift her spirits,' Felipe admitted. 'Señor Griego, your Pepita certainly did not write this letter out of a wish to marry Valenzuela. It was Miguel...'

'Miguel?' The old man struggled up onto his elbows, which evidently cost him quite a bit of effort. 'What of Miguel? Has something happened?'

'He is dead, señor,' Felipe said sadly.

'Valenzuela had him shot. But first he told Pepita that if she would write this letter to you, Miguel would be spared and would bring this letter to you himself. But Miguel has much honor, like you, señor. He refused to take the letter, even if Pepita wrote it. He said it would be a dishonor to him and to you and the whole Griego family, and he would prefer to die than dishonor the name of Griego. Pepita was afraid for him and said she would not allow him to die, and she wrote the letter to save his life. She has a good heart, señor. But Valenzuela gave Miguel no chance to change his mind, but ordered him shot immediately.'

The old man's hands bunched into weak but determined fists. 'That filthy scoundrel who calls himself a man! A mongrel dog who attacks his master is not as low as this dog Valenzuela. I will see Valenzuela dead. And I will most certainly not give my permission to Pepita to marry him, much less will I give her the gold mine for her dowry that I have promised her. Instead, I will find a way to rescue Pepita from the bandit's hands, and I will then attack his stronghold and vanquish him and all his men to the lower parts where they belong.' He breathed hard, and as though the speech had cost him a lot of strength. Then he added, 'I wish I was not under the rule of this disease of mine, or I would have long ago gone to deal with Valenzuela personally.'

'I have no doubt,' Felipe said.

After Griego had calmed down some, he rang for a servant and had the servant get a locked box from a safe in another room. Griego took a key from under his bedclothes and opened the box. He paid Felipe in gold. Then he indicated Clint.

'Is he deserving of money also? You have said he has saved your life. Have I him to thank for this information as well as yourself?'

Clint decided not to let on to know Spanish, in case Griego might be upset at having a stranger knowing about his troubles—you could never tell with Mexicans just what might upset them.

Apparently Felipe also thought this a good idea and without letting on either he translated the import of the questions into English.

'Tell him he can please himself, but that I'm not asking for anything,' Clint said in English, hoping that would be about the right attitude to please Griego.

Felipe translated it quite exactly, then added that it was his opinion that Clint deserved as much payment as himself, since they had been together all the way, and neither might have come through without the other. Griego then insisted on paying Clint in American gold coinage, twenty dollars. Clint made a show of being reluctant to take that much, and then thanked the rich old man through Felipe.

'Now then, Felipe,' Griego said in Spanish, when the transaction had been taken care of, 'here is another twenty for you. I have a message to write out for you to take to this bandit filth, if you think you can return there safely.'

'Of course,' Felipe told him. 'Valenzuela trusts me completely. He does not know that I work for you firstly and him only as a part of working for you.'

'That is good. Could you hand me that writing paper and the pen and ink, Felipe?'

As the old man wrote, his face grew dark and forbidding, and Clint was glad he was not the object of Griego's wrath, even with Griego a sick bed-ridden old man.

'There,' the old man said, as he fumbled at the paper, trying to fold it. Felipe took it from him and folded it, and helped Griego apply his seal. 'You take this to that filthy dog of a bandit. It will anger him, without doubt. You must be careful. It may cause him to strike out at the messenger for the message. It would not be beneath him. Will your friend be going with you?'

Felipe told him yes, and there was another small scene about money, Clint winding up with twenty more dollars.

'Well!' Griego said, once the business had been taken care of. 'And how is Adelita and the rest of the family?'

'They are fine, except for Adelita's illness, which you already know of.' Felipe gave Griego a long and detailed rundown on each of the children, and then went on to pass along news of other people in the family. Clint was getting the feeling that every Mexican was somehow related to every other Mexican, and half the gringos as well, though common sense told him it couldn't really be true. Clint fidgeted, chewing his toothpick into a mush of pulp and cleaning his nails with the point of his knife.

At last, Griego invited them to stay for a few days and enjoy themselves. But Felipe reluctantly refused, mentioning Valenzuela's desire for a reply in three weeks, almost two weeks of which had already passed.

'I am sorry to hear that,' Griego said. 'But at least you will stay the night?'

Felipe agreed to that, and they were shown to a couple of rooms. Clint was impressed with the one he was given. It was roomy, clean, with a massive oak bedstead. The bed was more comfortable than any he'd ever slept on.

Supper was the one unfortunate thing. For all his practice lately, he couldn't eat much of it. He sat around sipping wine made from grapes grown on the hacienda, and listening to a fellow named Mateo play the guitar. Mateo was quite good, and drew a lot of the house servants to listen.

When the evening was getting on, Clint and Felipe went off to their separate rooms. Clint, still feeling that he wasn't trusted, in spite of the old man's payment of forty dollars for his services, looked for a lock on the door, but found none. He put his pistol under the silk-covered pillow before settling in to go to sleep.

It was like floating in the air, and after all the weary riding he'd been doing recently, he didn't lie awake long . . .

. . . He was dreaming of burros. They were circling over his head like vultures, they were hidden out in the brush like Indians, and as soon as the sun came up . . . There was one somewhere in the room with him, he was sure, slipping around stealthily . . .

He came awake and in the darkness somewhere he heard the light scuff of a bare foot over the hardwood floor.

CHAPTER FOURTEEN

Clint listened hard for a few moments until he had a direction on the sound, and then leaped from the bed, gun in hand.

There was an answering scuffle as whoever was in the room with him headed for the door. Clint made a dive for the intruder, missed, and piled into a massive oak chest of drawers. As he was picking himself up, slightly dazed, the door closed and the running of padded feet retreated across the patio.

Clint yanked open the door and by the flickering light of a handful of oil lamps in brackets around the patio could make out a man darting into the shadows across the patio.

Clint, irritated and determined, darted into the patio after the man, following him through the zaguán and out into the open yard full of flower gardens. The sweet smell of jasmine was heavy on the night, and it felt like running through a thick fog to go through it. Clint could make out the running footfalls somewhere ahead and kept on.

The night exploded with muzzle flashes, and Clint dove for cover. The shooting stopped and the footfalls went on.

Clint came up from the flower bed he'd

flopped down in, running, gun in hand.

The night began to wake up. Guards came running, hammers of their guns clicking back. Casement windows opened, men called to each other in Spanish.

Clint thought about going on after the man who'd gotten into his room, and then thought about the kind of trouble that might buy for him, and against his powerful desire to find out who the man was decided he'd best light out for his room, and see if he could get there without showing himself. It was likely he wouldn't last the night, if he were found running around out here gunning for one of the hacienda's trusted men. This was a long way from home and mighty treacherous kind of country for an Americano. A smart man didn't push his luck.

He slid around through the bushes as men came charging down the garden paths to investigate the shooting. They all went by, and he trotted for the door of the house.

There were servants there, in their robes and wrapped in blankets. Clint held back in the shadows, thinking, waiting for these people to clear out so he could get in. But nobody was planning to budge until the excitement was over, that was clear. And Clint got to wondering what would happen if it was discovered he wasn't in bed where he belonged.

He considered acting as though he'd been first out to investigate the shooting, but figured nobody would believe him, since his room was on the far side of the patio and none of the people who came out of their own rooms to investigate would have seen him.

Clint had half a mind to hunt up his horse and make for the border, but that seemed an unlikely business, since he didn't even know where exactly the horses had been bedded down, and the vaqueros knew their ground a lot better than he did.

There was only one thing left, as far as Clint could see: go up over the roof somewhere at the back side of the building and climb down the latticework and slip along to his room.

It was hard to tell exactly what was going on down in the gardens, but everybody sounded plenty busy thrashing in the undergrowth, and Clint hoped they'd stay busy a while longer. He went along the wall to the left, following around two corners, and then hunted for a way up.

The wall was stone and adobe, massive construction. It was not perfectly smooth, but not rough enough to get handholds or footholds on. He wished he had a rope.

Some distance along the wall, he found a big oak tree with limbs that spread nearly over the roof. He climbed it and got cautiously out on the longest limb towards the building. The roof was ten feet down and five or six feet away. When he landed, he was going to make a clatter on that tile. But there was no way around it, and so he jumped.

He broke loose three tiles and they went skipping down the roof like bits of shale down a mountainside, ending up in the trough in the middle of the roof where rainwater collected to run along to a drain, under which was undoubtedly a cistern. Clint slid after the broken tiles into the trough and then listened. Off in the distance he could hear men talking. It sounded like the chase was over. Clint climbed up the other side of the roof and looked down into the patio. It was empty at the moment, but he could hear people in the portico, discussing the situation in rapid Spanish.

He found some latticework on which grew some vines, and climbed swiftly down to the stone floor of the patio. Then he darted through the shadows to his room and got into bed. Later, when everything had quieted down, he lit a candle and checked the room over. His knife, with his initials carved in the handle, was missing.

In the morning, Clint and Felipe were invited to have breakfast with Griego. Griego was still in his bed, but propped up. They were seated at a table by his bedside. Clint wondered how much he knew about what. They were served fruit, some of which Clint didn't even know the name for. But it was all welcome after the spicy food he'd been stuck with the previous night. It was smooth and fresh and he would have enjoyed it greatly if he hadn't been worried about what had happened the previous night.

Griego's eyes seemed to settle on him curiously every few minutes, as though waiting to see what he was going to say. Clint said nothing.

Felipe talked about his family some more, and then he and Griego both talked about the weather and about the danger from bandits that seemed to be everywhere. Griego's eyes clouded over with thunder heads as he talked about bandits.

Finally, Griego settled back against his pillows and eyed Clint with faint amusement. But he addressed Felipe when he spoke.

'I believe I have never told you, Felipe, of a small incident which happened not very long ago. I wished to hire an Americano who goes by the name of Clint Evans to rescue Pepita. It is said this Señor Evans is a very effective hunter of men and has done many amazing things. It is said he searches for a man who

134

killed his wife.' Griego was still looking at Clint, and Clint had a strong notion that Griego knew who he was.

'I sent a man to find Señor Evans and my man carried money to pay Evans this. This man never returned.'

'It is Valenzuela,' Felipe said with such conviction that if Clint hadn't known of Felipe's involvement he would never have suspected it. 'He has men everywhere. I do not think you will ever see this man again.'

'I do not expect it,' Griego said. And, still in Spanish, he addressed Clint. 'You have killed him, have you not, Señor Evans? And taken the money.'

Clint did not let on.

Felipe looked shocked and translated the accusation into English. Clint looked what he hoped was surprised and said, 'Tell him my name is Smith, and I can't understand what's put that notion into his head.'

When Felipe had translated, Griego's smile remained steady on Clint. His hand fumbled under the covers and pulled out Clint's knife.

'Señor Evans,' he said, 'I am well aware that you speak Spanish, and so I do not see any reason to trouble Felipe for translations. As you can see, I have your knife. Now you understand the disturbance last night. Let us not continue with this charade, eh?'

Clint looked back into Griego's eyes evenly, thinking. He had half a mind to put up a front of innocence, and hope Felipe would back him. But it would require long unconvincing explanations and in the end it was unlikely he'd ever convince Griego he was not Evans.

'It is a fine way to treat your guests,' he told Griego in Spanish.

'It is a fine way to treat a man who comes to hire you. It is beneath your dignity to kill such a man for money, is it not?' Griego's eyes were hard.

'I did not wish to become involved. I refused both the job and the money offered. There was shooting from the darkness, killing your messenger. I left. A man came after me and I killed him. Another man was after me also, but I got away.'

'And how is it you are here now with Felipe?'

'I am staying close to Felipe because I am hoping he can help me find Blake Dixon, who killed my wife.'

Griego smiled. 'Felipe has promised this?'

'Felipe has promised nothing. It is that he is my only hope of finding Dixon right now.'

'How is it you did not wish to rescue my daughter Pepita? The pay would be very high.'

'I do not like to become involved in family

quarrels.'

It appeared for a moment that Griego would explode at this way of referring to the kidnapping, but he contained himself and said softly. 'I will pay you as much as you desire, Señor Evans, if you will bring back my daughter alive and well.'

'It is not the money, Señor Griego. It is the lack of desire. I am sorry. I wish you well and my sympathies go with you, but I can not become involved in this.'

Griego closed his eyes and looked very old.

'I could have you killed, Señor Evans,' he said weakly. 'I could very easily think you killed Antonio and stole my money.'

'It would be a mistake,' Clint said flatly, leaving his meaning ambiguous.

Griego's eyes opened, and he looked sadly at Clint. 'Señor Evans, I care nothing for the life of one vaquero. I do not care if you have taken my money from him and in return have done nothing for it. I care only for my poor daughter who is in the hands of that bandit Valenzuela. If I considered that you would obey my orders and free her if I threatened your life, I would threaten it. But you need not fear, Señor Evans, I know enough of you to know that you would not scare so easily. You would be worse than useless in an attempt to rescue my daughter if you were not doing it because you wished to. Señor Evans, I must now appeal to your sense of right and decency and to your foresight of what will become of my daughter if she marries this dog. I am a very rich man, Señor Evans, I could afford to lose the mine which I have promised her as her dowry when she marries. It is not the wealth that concerns me. It is the man who will possess it, and worse, the man who will possess my daughter, against her will. Señor Evans, think of how it would be for you, if Pepita were your daughter. Would you be able to sleep or recover from your disease if your daughter were about to marry this scoundrel?'

'Well,' Clint said, 'if she does not wish to marry him, she could refuse—women change their minds all the time.'

'Valenzuela will not allow it. He will force her to submit.'

'Maybe I don't understand all this too well,' Clint said, 'but couldn't you stop the whole thing by just telling Valenzuela you won't give your daughter the mine if she marries him? It's the mine he's after, I'll wager. He's doing this to get his hands on it. But if you refuse to give it to her if she marries him, won't that stop it right there?'

Griego lifted a hand in exasperation, closing his eyes and shaking his head slowly from side to side as though in great pain.

'Señor, it is true you do not understand. I have given my word to Pepita that she will have the mine when she marries. It is known far and wide. I cannot go back on my word of honor. Would you, señor?'

'I would if it would get my daughter back.'

'I cannot. I have never in my life broken my word of honor.'

Clint shrugged. 'Well, I don't think just telling Valenzuela you're going to stop him if he tries to go through with his intention of marrying Pepita will do much but make him grin from one ear to the other.'

'It is true. This is the reason I must have your help. I could send some men to attack, but a battle would endanger Pepita's life. There is only one way to get my daughter out of there. A man such as yourself must find a route in and get her out by night over this route.'

Clint felt safe enough to refuse. 'I must tell you, Señor Griego, in all honesty, that there is no such way in or out. I have been into this stronghold of Valenzuela's, and it had only one way in and out, and this way is heavily guarded. There is no way at all to get your daughter out without the help of a large force of men, which you must have already. It is true that to attack would be dangerous to your daughter, but there is no other possible way. Even if I wish to help you, I could do nothing. I think you'd better forget your honor and let Valenzuela know he'll never get his hands on the mine.'

Griego lifted both hands to his face and then let them drop.

'There is also the problem that Valenzuela will be angry,' he said. 'If I did do that, he would kill Pepita out of spite. You are allowed in, are you not?' he asked. 'It is true you will be going with Felipe to deliver the message? Will you not consider while you are there, if there is not some way you might bring Pepita with you when you come out? I am not used to begging, señor, I never have in my life. But I beg you to help my daughter. If you succeed, I will give you all that you may wish.'

Clint fished out the twenty dollars he'd been given to help deliver the message, tossed it onto Griego's bed. 'I cannot promise even to do that,' he said. 'I have sent word to Dixon that I wish to see him. If I am offered an opportunity, I will see him and kill him. This may interfere with helping to deliver the message. I have no right to take money for a service I may not perform. However, if I do go with Felipe into the stronghold, I will consider how a rescue might be done. But I promise nothing. I will not myself be involved in a rescue. But if there is a way I can see it could be done, I will tell you how.'

Griego's expression relaxed. 'Oh, I am much indebted to you, Señor Evans. Keep the money. The peace of mind you have given me is worth much more than that. Please, take it, señor.'

But Clint refused, thinking of what was left of the other money belonging to Griego he carried. He felt a little guilty about it for the first time and would have returned it except that doing so would require too many difficult explanations he didn't feel safe trying to make.

CHAPTER FIFTEEN

They rode away over the rolling green hills of the hacienda's lush piece of Mexico, freshly supplied and sixty dollars richer between them. They passed small grazing herds of cattle which looked up munching as the men passed. Overhead the endless parade of summer clouds went by.

'I get the feeling you're related to any man who offers you money,' Clint commented to Felipe.

'The Señor Griego is my cousin also.'

'So I see. Which one *are* you working for?'

'I work for whoever will pay me, Cleent,' Felipe said with a grin. 'It does no harm, and I can support my family.'

'It'll catch up with you some day, Felipe, I'm telling you.'

'I have done this for many years.'

'This kidnapping has been going on for years?'

'Oh no. But there is always somebody who has a quarrel with somebody else, is there not? It is the way the world passes.'

'I still say it's risky.'

'But señor, you are doing it yourself, are you not? You have promised to look for a way to rescue Griego's daughter from Valenzuela.'

'I have promised nothing. I told him I'd take a look if I went with you and didn't get a chance at Dixon instead. I've got some sympathy for the old guy, and anyway, I didn't think I'd ever get him off my back if I didn't say something like that.'

'It was worth twenty dollars, was it not?' Felipe's eyes shone. 'You should have taken the money, Cleent. You could have made even more than that if you had wished. It is not difficult, once you know how. If you keep trying, you will learn.'

'Looky, Felipe Fats, if you want to live like a leech on other people's troubles, that's your business, but I have troubles of my own.'

'Sí, everybody has the troubles. I am not without troubles, señor. But there is much money to be made. When we see Valenzuela, he will probably desire us to return and convince Señor Griego that his daughter really desires of her own accord to marry Valenzuela. It will then be worth some more money to agree to this. Perhaps your ability to use the gun will become useful here, no? It is possible.'

'Did you get a chance to read Griego's letter before it got sealed?'

'I cannot read, señor, as you know.'

'Then it's like picking up a stick of dynamite without bothering to notice if the fuse is lit to go back to Valenzuela's stronghold. How do you know that Griego hasn't mentioned that you told him the real story of what happened to make Pepita write that letter?'

'Señor, I trust Señor Griego's intelligence. He knows that I am useless to him if he gives away that I work for him. It is the same with Señor Valenzuela. He will not say anything to Señor Griego that might make me useless to him.'

'You sure do think you've got everybody cornered just where you want them, don't you? But one day, you wait, it'll catch you when you aren't looking, and then you'll wish you'd never seen either one of these fellows in your life.'

'But Cleent, if you feel this way, why do you do it yourself?'

'I'm not. I can't seem to get it through your thick head. I told Griego exactly the truth. I don't like Griego much, but I like Valenzuela even less, and if Pepita doesn't want to marry him, I don't think she ought to have to. If there is no word from Dixon, then I'll have to go see Valenzuela and make him tell me where to find Dixon. And if I have to do that, I might as well take a look around and let Griego know if I see some way to get through the defenses. But I'm hoping it won't come to that. I'm hoping I'll get my hands on Dixon and see he pays for what he did to Margaret, and then ride for Colorado. And all without having to go near Valenzuela or Griego again.'

The ride north to Crooked Creek was uneventful, unless you counted the four times the burros got loose and ripped up their packs by crowding through thickets. The burros seemed to wander farther and farther at night, and the mornings searching for them grew long and tedious.

Crooked Creek was still roaring and buzzing with activity. As usual, there were several altercations going on at once. A pair of miners were hunkered down behind an ore wagon, hotly contesting something with two or three more behind a couple of water troughs across the street. The street in between was empty, but a couple of wagons that wanted to get by were pulled up short of firing range and their drivers were standing up waving their arms and their weapons and shouting angrily about disturbing the public's peace and obstructing the right-of-way.

Clint and Felipe pulled up behind, and just then the drivers of the wagons entered the fray, and pretty soon things were right lively there in the street.

'If you don't want your hair parted somewhere you don't like,' Clint said to Felipe, 'maybe we'd best ride around to the far end of town to get to Old Chap's.'

Felipe agreed, and they backed off and rode around outside town. Chap's was still standing, but was considerably more shot up since they'd been here last. Old Chap himself had his arm in a ratty sling and as they checked in he told them a tale of a general increase of excitement in these parts due to another strike. An argument about who the strike belonged to was still going on, but in the early stages it had taken place here at the hotel, and several patrons had been planted as a result. He himself had gotten winged when

145

he tried to clear the folks out before they brought the hotel down around everybody's ears.

'It was rather a fearsome fray, gen'lemen,' Old Chap said. 'We are used to a certain amount of shooting and disagreement among our patrons, but they had overstepped the bounds. I say, gen'lemen, you haven't by chance returned because of interest in the new find, have you? If you have, I'll thank you to discuss the merits of ownership in someone else's establishment.'

Clint assured him they would be careful not to be so rambunctious as to knock the building down, and then he and Felipe spread their rolls in the room they'd taken. They went out for supper, then returned. Clint had been in the habit of tying Felipe up at night during their trip north and now he had no intention of making any change just because they had reached Crooked Creek. Felipe had become stoical about this, finally realizing that all his running off when trusted spoke louder than his protestations of trustworthiness when the time of day came for him to be tied up.

Tonight, Felipe said, 'Cleent, I am thirsty. Let us have something to drink before we go to bed. We had not enough tequila on our travels.'

'Felipe, in the morning we have to get up

bright and early. I don't want you lying around holding your head until noontime. We're almost out of time now for getting to Valenzuela, remember?'

'Sí, this is true,' Felipe agreed mournfully. 'You are right. But perhaps one small drink could be allowed?'

'I guess one wouldn't hurt. I have to see if there's a message for me from Dixon anyway. Come on.'

After dark, the town was considerably more dangerous. Not because there were more bullets flying, or because there were more drunken miners in town, or because there was more card playing and hence more potential for disagreement—though all these things were true—but because it was dark and harder to see where bullets or knives or fists might come from. A wind blustered through the town lifting the grit and flapping the tents and howling in the ears and adding to the carnival atmosphere. Lanterns hanging inside the tents swung on their hooks as the tents worked, and threw the shadows of those inside against the tent walls in large wildly moving forms.

There were a lot of saloons, mostly in tents, with a board slung over a pair of hogsheads doing for a bar and apple crates of different sizes doing for tables and chairs. These places were packed full of whiskey-breathed miners,

147

bearded, fierce, with their belts full of knives and pistols and their scarred and rock roughened hands full of grimy cards. The whiskey was mostly of the rotgut variety, maybe a mixture of raw alcohol and creosote, enough to kill anyone not used to it, pretty near. It was served in a motley array of old tin cups and tankards. Glass wouldn't have lasted more than a couple of rounds in a place like Crooked Creek.

Clint, keeping Felipe at his side, asked in several of these saloons if there was any message from Dixon for him, and had no luck. Felipe then grew impatient and hauled Clint into a saloon that catered to the Mexican element. It was even dirtier and more makeshift than the saloons catering to Americanos. Felipe bought a drink and put it down like it was only a thimbleful of water. Before Clint could stop him, Felipe got down a second one. Clint tried to crowd to the bar to get Felipe by the arm, but this upset another fellow who spoke derisively of the pushy gringo and shoved him back. Clint had good reason not to get involved in a fight and so tried not to make an issue of it. He slid around and called to Felipe, reminding him he was only going to take one drink.

Felipe let on not to hear, or perhaps he really didn't. But the vaquero Clint had offended was spoiling for a fight, and he got Clint by the front of the shirt and yanked him close.

In Spanish, the man swore at him and called him a filthy gringo dog, and then hauled off to belt Clint. Clint ducked, and the fist hit someone behind him, and a yell went up, and the next minute, fists were swinging everywhere. Clint tried to push for the door. If he got himself laid out in a fight, he wouldn't be able to face Dixon successfully even if there was a message. But since he was the object of interest in this fight, he didn't get far before a fist landed solidly in his midsection, and the next thing he saw was the flash of a knife by the light of the swinging overhead lantern.

Clint got the wrist of the knife-wielding hand, and pushed the owner tumbling backwards into the crowd. This let him get another couple of feet towards the door, but then another fist glanced off his jaw, and for a moment everything got a little distant and hazy. He swung back, a kind of automatic reaction, and a knife flashed towards his arm, and before he could stop it, the blade sliced a hole in his shirt, the cold metal smooth and icy against his skin.

Clint tried to back away, but the man with the knife wanted him, and here it came again, driving upwards towards his belly.

Clint twisted sideways, finding that somebody had his arms from behind now. He saw grinning fierce Mexican faces, all waiting to watch the hated gringo writhe out his life on the knife.

Suddenly, he was scared. He realized he couldn't afford half measures any longer. He backed the crowd to one side with a powerful thrust of his legs, the knife gliding up his side, just drawing blood. He suddenly squatted and bent foward, breaking the grip of the man holding his arms. He drew his knife and came up again, the blade arcing in a quick flash into the other knife handler's wrist, drawing a scream and some blood and causing the Mexican's knife to fall. Clint's knife, flashing around, cleared space around him as the other Mexicans backed off.

This gave him gunning room, and he drew and cocked his gun, swinging it back and forth, glaring back into the fierce faces.

'Cuidado!' he bellowed warningly, and as he made for the door a path opened, respectful of the gun. He got outside and slipped off into the darkness. He found his legs were a little weak in the knees. All those damned Mexican faces had gotten to him.

For a moment it was silent in the tent, more or less, and then the place seemed to explode, and it wasn't half a minute before the tent collapsed on the yelling, swearing bunch of Mexicans, reducing the fight to a wriggle under a damper of canvas, until the smashed lantern suddenly flared up and set the whole thing on fire. Mexicans tore loose and ran off in all directions to leap into water troughs to cool off.

Clint kept his eye open for Felipe, and finally saw him staggering towards him, looking mighty scorched and cooked around the edges. Clint got him by the arm and yanked him hard towards the hotel. When they reached the room, Clint made sure Felipe was very well tied down to the bed.

'Hope you're satisfied,' Clint said.

'Sí, señor Cleent,' Felipe moaned. 'It is enough for one night.'

'Damned right it is,' Clint muttered.

He checked himself over, found he wasn't seriously hurt, though his shirt was getting to look a little flappy, and set off to finish making his rounds of the saloons.

He wasn't three steps out the door of the hotel when a pair of hulks came out of the dark and rammed their gun barrels into his back, one of them wanting to know, 'You Clint Evans?'

'I might know him,' Clint said cautiously, in case a yes answer might mean instant death.

'Never mind the clever talk. Is you or ain't you Clint Evans?'

'I don't talk good with guns in my back.'

'You better learn quick.'

Clint said, 'Looky, friends, I know this fellow Evans, I think. But I'm not mixed up with him. You don't want me. I just got here.'

'Check his pockets,' the other of the two men said with some disgust at his companion. 'You won't find out nothin' jawin'.'

Clint's pockets were searched, and a match struck to see what had been fished out. The knife was found with his initials on it.

'Okay, C.E.,' the first man said, jabbing the pistol barrel into Clint's back forcefully. 'That's close enough for me. The games is over. Let's go.'

CHAPTER SIXTEEN

Clint kept looking for a chance to get the upper hand, but it never came. He was put into the back of a buckboard and tied up. The two men got onto the seat and one of them sung out to the horses and away they went, jouncing and clattering over the rough ground, going east out of town, as near as Clint could tell. He couldn't sit up because his wrists were tied back to his ankles, behind him.

He wasn't long figuring that Dixon had gotten his message and this was the answer. Dixon must have long known why Clint wanted to find him, if he had ears everywhere. Probably he'd just smiled to himself at the puny efforts of the bereaved man to find him. But now, perhaps he was worried for some reason, or maybe it was an amusement to him to play with Clint.

The stars looked solemn and peaceful way up there. Clint couldn't see anything else for the sides of the buckboard. He wondered if Felipe was this uncomfortable. Filipe could have prevented the necessity for being tied up though, by being trustworthy. Clint didn't feel sorry for him.

The buckboard jounced on and on. The night passed slowly, the stars grew pale and tired after the long night and lost some of their piercing sharpness, then disappeared altogether as the sun came up and made a bright hard glare of the sky. The men halted and ate something, took a swig or two from a jug of forty rod, and then, ignoring the prisoner, went on driving the buckboard, talking about whiskey they'd drunk and women they'd had and gold they'd found and fights they'd fought, each fellow trying to outdo the other, the tales getting taller and taller, and gaudier and gaudier.

They had gotten to where one fellow had just told how he'd killed thirty-five Mexicans and ten Indians in one morning and was about to tell about what he'd done at Kate's over to Dry Diggings, where there were twenty-five girls ready and willing, when the other fellow told him to cork up and meditate on his lying nature, they had arrived.

Clint, sore and tired from the long painful sleepless ride, was cut loose and jostled out of the buckboard onto his feet.

They were nowhere, unless you could call the broken down Conestoga wagon sunk in the sand somewhere. The wagon had about half the canvas cover left, bleached a hard white by the sun, torn and frayed by the wind. A pair of horses were tethered off in the brush a ways, and that was it. Just desert and sky in all directions.

Clint mopped at his neck with his bandana and found his arm and hand had to work hard to do that much. He was given a chance to relieve himself and did so. Then he was led to the rear of the Conestoga wagon.

Sitting calmly in the shade of the cover, like people in other parts sat under awnings and watched life go by, were two men, a cold-eyed, well-dressed fellow, and a bodyguard type bristling with pistols, knives, spurs, teeth and the points of a waxed mustache.

The cold-eyed man looked with curiosity at Clint, running his eyes down and up his length like a man sizing up a horse.

'So you're Evans,' he said mildly. 'You wanted to talk to me? Important, I think you said.'

Clint sized up the other a moment, and then said, 'Dixon?'

'Who did you figure?' Dixon was amused. His sidekick was not, and kept his dour watchful look, like a man who's just tasted his meat and suspects it's more maggots than beef.

Clint didn't figure Dixon for anything better than totally treacherous, but he was thinking too much of how his dead wife had looked to think sensibly and be cautious.

'I'm here to kill you,' Clint said. 'Because of my wife.'

'What the hell are you talking about?' Dixon almost managed to look really surprised and puzzled.

'Never mind playing innocent. Five years ago, before you got rich, you decided to have some fun. You found my wife alone in the house and took her off into the woods. I found her naked and battered to death. I'm saying this not to remind you, but to let your friends here know the kind of man you are, in case they don't know already.'

Dixon's face twisted into a cynical grin. 'You have a notion to stand off the whole bunch of us with nothing but your fists?'

'I'll do that if I have to. You don't have any self-respect at all?'

Dixon laughed.

'You mean honor? You want to fight it out, man to man? Don't be foolish. Only cowboys and Mexicans talk about honor. Fools. Why should I give you a chance to kill me? I've fought long and hard to get where I am. Why should I take any risks I don't need to? For you it's too late, but I'll give you a piece of advice anyway. It you want to get anywhere, you must not take any unnecessary risks. Any man of sense knows he cannot afford honor.'

He got up and stepped into the sun. 'Well, boys, I'll bet you could do with some fun, eh? Just keep an eye on him while I get my horse.'

Dixon mounted up and adjusted his rope in his hand. A moment later he set his heels, rope flying over his head, and Clint ducked aside as the rope whistled out.

The three henchmen laughed and pushed Clint out away from the cover of the wagon, grins on all their faces. Clint took his opening and ran.

So what the hell had he expected Dixon to

do? Fight him a fair fight?

He had not planned on giving Dixon that opportunity. He had planned to kill Dixon slowly, making sure he hurt plenty for his crimes.

There were only a few small clumps of mesquite dotting the area around the wagon, not much cover. Clint headed across the seventy yards of open space for the nearest of them, Dixon whirling his horse to come after him, swinging his loop.

Clint saw he wasn't going to make it, and as the loop sailed out towards him, he cut from under it, darting behind Dixon's back and continuing for the mesquite.

He made the mesquite this time, and dove under its thorny branches getting scratched but not really noticing. It was only a momentary shelter, he knew that. But he needed time to think. What he needed was to get the other horse. That would at least give him a chance to get away. But the dun was forty yards off, and Dixon was prancing his black back and forth yipping and yelling in between.

The loop lashed out, settled around the mesquite bush and Dixon set his spurs. The bush thrashed wildly while the audience yelled encouragement. The mesquite snapped and twisted and then it was gone, bouncing along behind Dixon's horse. Clint, sprayed with sand, blinked at what had gotten into his eyes and rolled to his feet, figuring to make use of what time he had to get to the dun.

Dixon had to get down from his black to get his rope off the mesquite bush. Clint, breathing hard and sweating in the sun, got most of the way to the dun before the men watching saw what he was up to and yelled. Dixon spun on his heel, drawing, and sent lead whizzling past Clint's ears.

He still had distance to go to get to the dun and figured he might die before he got there, and so dove for the cover of another thicket, this one bigger, but scrawny and thin. Dixon was back on his horse again, and here he came, swinging his loop and yelling.

He thrashed right into the thicket, mercilessly kicking his horse through the brambles, plunging at Clint. Clint scrambled out the far side and started around towards the dun again, but Dixon was out quicker than Clint had figured and suddenly he realized that with Dixon between him and cover, he had nowhere to run.

The loop licked out again, Clint managed to dodge, again, and he felt it hit him on the head. The third time Dixon guessed correctly which way Clint would cut and the loop dropped neatly over him, tightened pinning his arms to his sides, and then tugged him backward onto his butt, and he was being dragged along the ground.

It wasn't pleasant, but it was bearable, until Dixon spurred into a bed of cactus. Clint felt the spikes of the cactus tear his clothes then his flesh, and gritted his teeth, trying to roll onto his feet. He knew if he didn't get there in a few seconds, he would be so ripped up he'd bleed to death in only a few minutes, with Dixon and his crew standing around watching and laughing.

He timed a bounce and got his feet under him, running after the horse, working hard to stay on his feet. He'd never been given back his knife, or his pistol, and so had only his hands to work with. He tried to run fast enough to take the tension out of the rope, but Dixon saw he was on his feet and spurred his horse on faster, heading through the cactus bed again. Clint tripped and fell.

Spikes ripped at him from all sides, and he tried again to get to his feet, but his head hit something hard and he blacked out.

CHAPTER SEVENTEEN

He woke up thinking of burros and Mescaleros, and then wondered what he was doing looking up at the bright glare of the midday sky. His eyes hurt to look at it and he closed them again, and wondered why he felt uncommonly pained all over and dizzy and didn't seem to have any strength.

He remembered and groaned, and struggled cautiously to sit up, feeling light-headed. Searing pain yelled out all over him as crusted scabs cracked open.

He was alone. At least as far as he could tell. He heard nothing, saw nothing—except a couple of carrion birds drifting around interestedly away up there over his head. He felt irritated and tried to shake his fist at them, but the pain was so great, he soon gave up that effort and lay back, figuring he was done.

'It is the way the world passes, no?' he muttered aloud, mimicking Felipe.

Thinking of Felipe, he thought of all those Mexicans who had surrounded him in the saloon, wanting to see him die, and thinking of them made him think about how he had come to the point he was at now, dying in the desert. If he died, Dixon would win.

160

That annoyed him. In fact it made him damn mad. Dixon deserved to die. He deserved to die in the most horrible way imaginable.

Clint decided he wouldn't just lie here and die. He was going to see that Dixon paid for what he'd done. If there had been any doubt before whether torture was right for Dixon, there was none now. Clint made up his mind he had no reason to feel guilty about his plans for Dixon.

He opened his eyes and struggled up to a sitting position again and began to take stock. His shirt didn't amount to anything but a few shreds, and likewise his pants, though they were a little better. His boots were still intact, more or less. He did not see his pistol or knife left around for him anywhere, and his money was gone. The wagon was empty, and so were the bushes where the horses had been tethered, and the buckboard was gone. He guessed from the look of his bloody body and the stains in the sand that he had lost a fair amount of blood. It seemed likely that he'd lose a lot more without considerable bandaging and three or four weeks in bed with somebody seeing to his wants. It also seemed likely he was going to have to do without these luxuries, for the most part, for some time. He might be able to make a few bandages out of what was left of his clothes, but if he lay around here very long the buzzards were going to have a feast in a short while.

Very very gingerly he prodded and tested and found where the worst leaks were and then with a great deal of moaning and groaning due to the pain, he got what was left of his shirt off and made into a sort of generalized bandage that went around his chest and back, where the worst rents in his skin were. He also tugged out a few of the more obvious thorns stuck in him, so as to keep the further aggravation of the wounds to a minimum. Then, fortified with the bandage and with the knowledge that he had no choice, he began trying to get onto his feet.

This took him what seemed like ten years, all of it spent in the lower regions of the place below, but at last he managed it, and weaved around in his dizziness, having no confidence he was going to be able to remain standing long, let alone start walking.

But after a little while, his head got used to working in an upright position, and the pain sort of dulled down and became a generalized throb.

Clint peered around the horizon and wondered which way he ought to go. If his guess had been right, and they had taken him east of Crooked Creek, then the thing to do was go west, follow the sun, which was now getting well along on its way to the horizon. It was a long walk, but there was nothing he knew of in the other direction for a good long way, like fifty miles, and with his doubtful sense of navigation out here he might ride for a week on a good horse and never see anything, unless it was Mescaleros out to scalp him.

So, finally, he set off. The first hundred yards was the most terrible kind of torture and Clint became certain that there was no kind of terror hell could hold for him worse than what he went through those first hundred yards.

But since he had no choice but keep walking or die—and let Dixon get away with his crimes—he walked. He sustained himself partly by telling himself how he would take it out of Dixon's hide, planning the details.

The second hundred yards was a lot easier. The wounds that were going to open, had, and the pain became a general throb that little by little receded into a kind of weariness. His mind became blank, plans for Dixon receded. He trudged on, following the sun down, and then feeling the relief of the evening cool coming on as it set and the desert fell dark.

He stopped not too long after dark, but an hour later when he tried to get going again the pain was so bad and he felt so weak that he resolved not to stop again, until he either found the town or other refuge, or died.

He walked all night and by now was moving slowly, tongue lolling with thirst. He stopped again because he couldn't keep going. Then, after another two hour break, he started moving again. The pain was terrible, but somehow it seemed removed, like it was really somebody else's pain this time and he was just hearing the screams.

He managed to keep going all day, even in the heat of the noontime furnace. He wanted to stop all the time, but knew if he did this time he'd never get up again.

Night fell, and he estimated that he should have come almost far enough to fetch the town, but he couldn't hear anything on the southwest wind, nor smell anything either.

He kept moving, going more and more slowly, all night, and by now was feeling that if in the morning the Mescaleros came for him it would be a blessed relief.

The next day, at about midmorning, he collapsed and blacked out, thinking vaguely that he'd sure given it a try anyway.

He woke up stiff and dry and hungry and so tired it took five tries to get onto his feet. He would have fallen down again and been all done right there, he was sure, if he hadn't happened to look southwest and see a lone brush hut.

Felipe's?

He was confused but didn't worry too much about that. He saw hope for himself and made for the hut. It took most of the morning for him to labor the relatively short distance, and he kept wondering why nobody came out or moved around the area. It was Felipe's, he was sure. He recalled that odd looking rock over there, and the lay of the ground.

Overhead circled buzzards, and Clint made a hoarse sound of defiance, thinking that he was going to outwit them after all. With a final effort he fell across the doorstep and onto the packed floor in the shade of the hut. He looked vaguely at all of Felipe's family sitting or lying around and wondered at their lack of surprise and then let go and fell asleep.

$$\star \quad \star \quad \star$$

He woke up and found his vision blurry. When it cleared, he looked at the group of people sitting and lying around him and was still amazed at their lack of reaction to him being there.

Then he was even more startled to see that nobody seemed to budge at all, or say anything.

There was a flapping in the doorway, and a

searing pain in his leg as claws dug in. He jerked at the pain, and with a raw edged call, the buzzard flapped away out of the doorway, to stand around looking hurt a short way off.

Clint struggled up into a sitting position. Flies roared. There was a lot of blood.

They were all dead.

CHAPTER EIGHTEEN

Clint had been at Felipe's for three weeks, nursing his wounds, eating what food had been left, drinking water that had to be hauled from a tinaja some distance away, before he had the strength to do more than cover the bodies with mats and a few rocks. It had taken him two days of recovery to get to the water, and it was only on the third day that he found energy enough to cover the bodies. He mostly stayed outside the hut, in its shade, because of the smell and the flies.

Now he used an old shovel he found in a corner to dig a large grave, and he hauled the bodies, what was left of them, buzzing with flies and crawling with insects and larvae, to it and dumped them in. He was glad to get them underground and let the hut air out.

He made himself something to eat and sat in

the shadows of the hut's doorway watching the night come on.

He had been sitting there for some time, feeling for the first time in a long time a sense of well-being, wondering if it was the Mexican clothes he'd found to wear that made him feel cooler and more comfortable here in the desert or whether it was just that he was getting used to the heat finally—when there was a clatter of pebbles and the nicker of a horse.

Clint, having no weapon, slid into a nook he'd made in the thick brush wall of the hut, and waited.

'Adelita!' Felipe's voice sung out gaily. 'Adelita, my darling sweet rose, my pretty flower of the desert! I have brought you a present!'

Clint slid out of his nook and out the front door.

'Hola, Felipe,' he said.

'Cleent?' Felipe jolted in surprise. 'It is good to see you, Cleent! But what are you doing wearing the clothes of Mexico, señor? Have you decided to become part of my family?' Felipe was wary.

'Get down, Felipe. I've got bad news for you.'

'Oh, señor, have compassion. You leave and you do not come back. I look for you, Cleent, but I do not find you. I swear on my mother's holy grave that I search, Cleent. I am afraid you are killed and I ask everywhere, but you are gone.'

'Forget it, Felipe. It isn't that. Come around here with me a minute. I've got to show you something.'

'But Señor Cleent,' Felipe said, 'I will be glad to go with you, but first I must speak to my wife and my children. Why do they not come out to greet me? Adelita! José, Francisco! María!'

'They're dead, Felipe,' Clint said bluntly.

Felipe was dead silent for a moment.

Then he said softly, 'Dios mío.'

He slid slowly off his horse and came to look into the hut, as though he expected to see them all lying there.

'I've buried them just today,' Clint said. 'That's what I wanted to show you.'

Felipe spent a long time by the grave, and Clint heard him praying off and on in Spanish.

* * *

The desert lit up with a bolt of lightning like a jagged rent in the sky letting in the fires of hell beyond, and then came a rumbling of thunder. The sky lit up again, then again, the thunder roaring and booming off around the desert like the place was full of artillery fighting a war.

The rain came suddenly, in a furious torrent that inside of five minutes was rushing in the wash just down over the rise on which the hut stood. Inside of ten minutes, water was rushing through the hut itself, just as though the hut had been built in the middle of a stream. Felipe had still not come in.

Clint was about to go out and see if Felipe had been washed away when the fat Mexican came waddling through the door and sat down with a splash in the flowing water.

Clint had lit a stump of candle, but the water pouring in through the nearly worthless thatched roof had put it out. Now Clint decided to try again. He thought it might make Felipe feel better. He found a poncho and propped it over the candle, which he'd set in a crook of the brush which made the wall, and lit it again. This time it did not go out.

They were silent for a long time. Clint wasn't going to disturb Felipe's thoughts at a time like this. Clint might find a lot of fault with the fat Mexican, and he might not trust him, but Felipe had cared about his family, and Clint liked Felipe for that.

The candle had almost burned out, and the storm had quit and the water stopped running through the hut when Felipe finally spoke.

'I did not think Valenzuela would let out his

169

rage with me upon my family,' he said sadly, broodingly. 'I was thinking I was very smart to get away. I wished to celebrate my victory and share it with Adelita. I went to town and bought her a new dress. It is very pretty, Cleent. It would have made her very happy. She would have forgotten her sickness and she would have been full of joy.'

Clint said nothing.

'It passed as you warned me it would,' Felipe went on. 'Valenzuela he reads the message and is very angry. He calls me many names, and says I have told Señor Griego that the letter is not the way Pepita really feels. Then he locks me in the small jail building and says I am to die soon. Many days pass. Juan Carlos who is the guard is Adelita's uncle. I soften his heart and finally he lets me get away, telling the other guards that I am allowed to leave. He leaves with me, because he will die if he stays. I have to leave the burros, but I have my horse and my gun and my money from Señor Griego. I am free and I feel fine. So I am very gay when I come home. I am looking forward to the big smile on Adelita's face when she sees the present I have bought her. I am imagining how she will laugh and chatter and try the new dress on and how she will wish to dance and sing and be merry in the way she did many years ago. I am

170

imagining how my house will be bright and full of laughter when I come and it will be time for Adelita's saint's day soon and I will go to town and buy more things, and much tequila.'

Felipe paused and looked around the empty hut.

'It is the way the world passed,' Clint said, and then wished he hadn't because he sounded as though he was mocking Felipe.

'Sí,' Felipe said. 'Sí. But it is not right. Señor Valenzuela had no right to kill my family. It is an abomination. It is the act of a scoundrel dog, a cowardly yellow filth.' Felipe's eyebrows lowered and in the candlelight he looked dangerous, the first time Clint had ever seen this expression on Felipe's face.

'Not much you can do,' Clint said.

'Do you think I will do *nothing*? Of all people you should know how I feel, Señor Cleent. My life is full of sadness and emptiness now. And it is all because of the filthy cowardly act of Valenzuela.' Felipe got up and went to the door of the hut, looking out at the blackness. 'Señor Cleent, I am going to kill Valenzuela.'

Clint said nothing for quite a while. He had been doing some thinking about his own situation over the past three weeks, and had

171

come to the conclusion that the only way to get Dixon would be to take him by surprise in his own lair. Clint was sure he'd never stand a chance of getting the upper hand otherwise. And since Valenzuela was the only man Clint knew of who might know where Dixon went to ground, it seemed the only thing to do was get hold of Valenzuela and make him talk.

'Looky, Felipe,' he said at length. 'I had no luck at all getting at Dixon the way I tried. I nearly got myself killed for my trouble. I haven't shown you, but I'm all over ripped up by thorns from a trip through a cactus bed behind Dixon's horse. Dixon was too arrogant to make sure I was dead before he and his henchmen rode off and left me, so here I am. But I'm no further ahead than I was before. Leaving word again would just make me open to another attack and a repeat of what I just went through. But Valenzuela knows where Dixon hides out. If I can get him in his own lair . . .'

Felipe turned to face him, the sputtery candle throwing queer shadows over his face.

'Señor, we are united. We have a common purpose. This time there will be no need to worry that I will abandon you. We both wish something from Valenzuela. First you will ask him where Dixon is, and then I will kill him. Perhaps I will have to begin to kill him before he will tell you the truth, eh?' Felipe's teeth looked yellow and fierce as he grinned. He was no longer the Felipe of only a few hours ago, calling gaily for his wife.

'The problem we have,' Clint said, 'is how to get to Valenzuela.'

Felipe came in and sat down. 'Sí, Cleent, that is our problem. It will not be easy.'

'It'll be damned hard.'

'But we will do it, eh? I wish to see Valenzuela's blood run freely and to hear his screams as I tear out his eyes.'

CHAPTER NINETEEN

They had not come up with a plan by the time they went to bed. But the reason Clint couldn't sleep wasn't really that. It was Felipe's attitude. The image of Felipe's yellow teeth stayed with him.

In the morning Felipe set off to gather some herbs and Clint hauled more water. They took a siesta at noon which lasted most of the rest of the day while they talked about Valenzuela and worked over many different possible plans to get their hands on him.

By the time they took to their bedrolls that night they had merely begun to realize just

173

how hard it was going to be to get hold of Valenzuela. For four more days they argued and discussed and suggested and argued some more.

By the end of the fifth day, however, they had come to one clear conclusion: they needed help. The next question to be answered was, what kind of help and who would they try to get it from?

For a couple more days they argued about this. Then, as the sun set on the second day, they stopped talking, and a grim determination settled over the hut in the desert. They went to bed silent and each full of his own thoughts. In the morning, exchanging only a few words, they collected their belongings, saddled their horses and rode for Crooked Creek to put into action the plan they had hammered out.

*   *   *

Crooked Creek seemed quieter than usual when they rode in. Maybe the ranks of the impatient and argumentative had been temporarily thinned out and there was a lull until more could ride in from elsewhere to take their places. This wasn't to say the place was all sweetness and light. There was a brawl going on desultorily in a saloon they passed, and up the street a man was waving his arms and yelling at somebody inside one of the tents about something Clint couldn't make out.

They used some of their pooled money to buy a couple of burros and some supplies for a trip. As the afternoon began to cool just slightly, they rode south into the desert.

They hadn't joked or complained about each other since coming to a decision about what they would do. They spoke only when necessary and about practical things. Each was full of his own thoughts. Clint kept watching Felipe and wondering at the change that had come over him. He had turned into a grim bloodthirsty man, and he was obviously brooding all the time about what he was going to do to Valenzuela when he got his hands on him. Every little while a sort of fierce glare of pleasure would come over Felipe, and Clint figured Felipe had just finished an imagined torture of Valenzuela.

Clint was silent and brooding too, but for a different reason. He kept wondering if he wanted to have any part of Felipe's torture of Valenzuela. Valenzuela probably deserved it, but Felipe's attitude made Clint uneasy.

They rode onto the lush green ranges of the Griego hacienda towards noon of another fine bright day—there'd been no more gully washers since that one back at the hut. The

175

place looked about the same, creamy white buildings etched against the dark green backdrop of the lower slopes of the massive Sierra Madre, the little parades of summer clouds with wind-streaked bottoms going by overhead, the little clumps of healthy fat cattle feeding on the ranges, the sombreroed vaqueros working the range.

Felipe had few pleasant words for the man who took their horses and wanted to know how was Felipe and all the family? They went inside and were shown to the old man's room. He had been asleep and was bleary-eyed when they came in. But when he saw Felipe and Clint he smiled hopefully.

'Ah, I knew my faith was not misplaced,' he said in his clear well-spoken Spanish. 'My friends have come back. You have good news?'

Felipe stood at his bedside like an angry bear, working his hands. Clint unconsciously stuck a toothpick in the corner of his mouth.

'I have news,' Felipe said forebodingly. 'My family has been killed.'

Griego looked shocked. 'Oh, my good friend Felipe! This is terrible! Who has done this horrible thing?'

'Valenzuela.'

Griego's brows jutted at that, and thunderclouds formed back in his dark deep set eyes. 'It is to be expected from such a filthy dog.'

'I am going to tear out his eyes and cut him into small pieces,' Felipe said darkly. 'I'm going to make him repent his sins many times over and beg for his life and scream in horrible pain. I will have no mercy.'

Griego's eyes flashed. 'I have the same wishes, Felipe, I assure you. I wonder if I am not responsible though for causing this to happen. I should not have sent you into the den of that worthless pitiless animal. Even though I did not mention that you told me the truth behind Pepita's letter, I am sure Valenzuela suspected it, and I feel responsible, Felipe. You have come here with your friend, the Señor Evans. Have you come to me for help?'

'That's right,' Clint said. 'We looked at it from every angle, and finally agreed we needed help. You were the only man who had an interest in getting the best of Valenzuela besides us. You have a lot of men, and could afford to supply a small army.'

'What is your need to destroy Valenzuela?' Griego asked.

'I don't care about Valenzuela. But he is the only man who knows where Blake Dixon hides out. I want Dixon. So we've got to work this so I get a chance to make Valenzuela talk before Felipe gets his time with him. Your interest is to get your daughter out safely, so you will not have Felipe's temptation to destroy Valenzuela's stronghold without discrimination.'

Griego nodded thoughtfully. He looked stronger now than he had before. Perhaps for the first time he thought he saw light at the end of the tunnel.

'Señor Evans, that is why I wanted to hire you in the first place, because an army, no matter how large, could not rescue my daughter. I am very willing to help you and your friend Felipe here, for I have much the same feelings towards that filth Valenzuela. But I do not see what good an army will do. I will supply it however, if you think it is necessary.'

'It is. But this won't be a simple attack. Felipe and I have worked out a plan. Your force will be mostly a diversion.'

'I am afraid that I do not understand,' Griego said.

So Clint laid it all out for him.

Griego listened carefully, nodding at some points, shaking his head at others, and then afterwards was silent for the space of several minutes.

'It is very brilliant, Señor Evans,' he said softly. 'My confidence in you is not

178

misplaced. You have a good brain. However, there are weaknesses. It could go wrong.'

'It could. If you have a better idea, let's hear it.'

Griego shook his head, smiling wanly. 'No, Señor Evans, I have no better plan. I do not like playing games with the life of my daughter, and I do not like risks. But I am not fool enough to believe there is a way out of this situation that does not have risks. I give my blessing. I will order that you have one hundred and forty men, together with all the supplies and ammunition needed. And I will pray that God in His Holy Wrath will be with you to punish this evil coward, and to rescue my innocent daughter from his clutches.'

They remained at the Griego hacienda for three days while the army was put together, supplied and provisioned for the nearly two week journey north to Oak Creek. Clint and Felipe were given the royal treatment, fed the finest foods and wines and treated to music and dancing. A peculiar kind of atmosphere was on the hacienda. It was a sort of fierce fiesta, like an Indian war dance, grim with the determination to kill the enemy and rescue Pepita. Felipe muttered in his sleep and Clint said little, pondering the business.

They set out on another in the long succession of bright mornings, looking like a bunch of revolutionaries. Every man had crossed shoulder belts of ammunition, and pistol and knife handles protruded in profusion everywhere on the sombreroed, hard-faced Mexicans. Their hearts were in this battle, that was clear. It was perhaps as well that they did not know how small a part they were supposed to play, or perhaps they wouldn't have looked forward so much to what they were riding into. Griego commanded loyalty, Pepita reverence, and Valenzuela the most concentrated and furious hatred.

They rode all day, with only a relatively short stop at the noon siesta time. That night, Clint sat looking at the campfires sprawling over the desert and felt the night breeze on his cheek and listened to the quiet talk. There was no laughter or joviality as usually filled Mexican camps in the evening. This was a grim determined business, and Clint realized he was part of it. He had a hankering to pull out and back off and think about it, but it was in motion now, and he wanted Dixon and this was the way to get him. What these Mexicans did to each other was no concern of his.

Later, somebody got out a guitar and played, and soon another man began to sing, the cry lonely and mournful and Clint thought of the rows of empty weathered buildings in

Dead Flats, and remembered the Presence stalking the streets. The camp was silent, listening, but way out in the desert somewhere a coyote joined in, howling and yipping. When the singer finally stopped singing about a tragic love affair and the other man put away his guitar, the coyote yipped a few times and quit too.

And all that was left was the tickling of the sand as the wind filled all the tracks of the day and left the avengers alone on a trackless desert.

CHAPTER TWENTY

The ride north was uneventful. Clint thought maybe the Mescaleros were taking a vacation or had moved to better hunting grounds. Oak Creek was reached without anyone seeing a single Indian. Clint and Felipe decided on a spot along the creek under the oak trees to make camp. There was good visibility in all directions and the oak trees would make for some cover, if they needed it.

They had arrived in the middle of the day, so Clint and Felipe decided to make use of the afternoon putting the next step of the plan into motion. They rode together the mile into town and cast about for an appropriate saloon. It had to be one they might conceivably have both gone into. They found a dingy little place not too far from the wall of cliff down which the ore from the mines poured. The rumble of it made everybody have to raise his voice to be heard.

Clint and Felipe stood for a moment in the entrance, and then Clint pointed at an old man sitting alone at a table in the corner, watching them with bright eyes. He was dressed like an old-time trapper, but fallen on hard times. They sat down at the table across from him, he watching them all the way, saying nothing.

'You like a drink?' Clint asked him.

'Why, I reckon.'

'Redeye?'

'Sure.'

When they all had redeye before them, Clint asked, 'You been around here a while?'

The old fellow chuckled. 'I reckon for just a *little* while, not more'n fifty or a hundred year though. That long enough for ye?'

'You know these parts?'

The old fellow laughed some more. 'I reckon I can find my way home when I have to.'

'Looky,' Clint said, glancing around as though to see if they were being watched, 'you know if there's some place hereabouts grazing

182

bighorns?'

'Well, there may be. But I cain't say's I've ever seed one anywheres near this far south.'

'You're sure? We're ready to pay a hundred dollars to the man can show us some bighorns. Money in advance.'

'Wal, my memory's a-goin', and my eyes isn't so good no more, but it do seem to me as I'm fairly sure they ain't sich critters round about here.'

'That so,' Clint said, acting disappointed. 'Me and my friend here, we had our hearts set on shooting some of them bighorns, you know? But I guess if there aren't any, then there aren't any.'

They drank their drinks.

'Much obliged,' Clint said, getting up.

'Sure thing,' the old fellow said genially.

Clint had seen another fellow, this one a man of doubtful profession, bellying to the bar. Clint figured him for the next mark. Clint and Felipe braced the man and told the same story. This fellow, named Joe Lang, offered to show them where there were some sheep up in the mountains not far away, and Clint decided this fellow was enough of a possibility to accept the offer. They agreed to meet back at this saloon the next morning at daybreak, ready to ride after sheep.

As they rode back to their camp, Felipe

said, 'Well, Cleent, it is very hard to tell with him, is it not? Perhaps he is one who will betray or perhaps he is not.'

'Well, agreeing to show us sheep we know don't exist is a good start. We'll just have to see if he'll sell us out or not.'

★   ★   ★

The following morning at the agreed time Felipe and Clint were waiting at the saloon door. Joe Lang rode up on a shoddy-looking horse, without a rifle but wearing a pistol. There was a bedroll on his cantle.

'Ready, gen'lemen?' he asked.

'Let's go,' Clint said.

'The money?'

Clint passed it over. The man counted it, shoved it into a pocket. Then swung his horse and led off.

They rode along without talking for quite a while, winding through the lush canyons and gullies, on the trail towards Valenzuela's stronghold.

'There's a lot of places you could go,' Lang said tentatively. 'You have a hankerin' for high places or the valleys?'

Clint eyed him and decided now was as good a time as any to make the next move.

'Well, Mr. Lang, I'm going to ask you man

184

to man. Can I trust you?'

Lang's face started into a fox-like smile that flashed off immediately.

'I reckon so,' he said.

'We aren't after bighorn sheep.'

'That so,' Lang said noncommittally.

'Fact is, we aren't hunting.'

'That right?' Lang responded. He was concentrating on rolling a cigarette.

'You know Valenzuela?'

The man started slightly, but covered by acting as though he had an itch.

'I heard of him.'

'Know where his hideout is up here?'

Lang tucked the cigarette into the corner of his mouth and looked at them. Clint realized he'd made it hard for the man, since Lang didn't know if he should admit to knowing or not.

'Looky, Mr. Lang,' Clint went on. 'My friend here and I are not alone. We have a force of about a hundred and forty men, with plenty of guns and the lead to push through them. Camped down on the flats by the creek southeast of town. We're here to take Valenzuela's stronghold. We'll pay you another hundred dollars to show us the lay of the land all around the stronghold. And keep quiet about it.'

Lang puffed on his cigarette. 'I can show

you,' he said.

'Good.'

Lang led them for two days around the steep rocky trails that skirted the massive chunk of rock which held the hollow that Valenzuela was using as his stronghold. Clint became worried about how to set up an attack on this place that would seem a real threat to Valenzuela. Simply storming the place would be nearly impossible. The rock was like an oversized boulder sitting on the mountainside. There was only the one crack which gave access to the hollow inside. The outside of the boulder was otherwise straight-sided and sheer, about a hundred and fifty to two hundred feet high. Once in a while they caught glimpses of men patrolling way up there. There were undoubtedly a good many men up there, and anybody trying to climb up could be picked off with the greatest ease at the leisure of the men on top, who could take it in casual turns, the off watch drinking tequila or pulque or whatever and holding a fiesta.

Once they had been all the way around the rock and Clint had asked all the right questions of Lang, they all rode back to town, Clint paid the guide his hundred and then he and Felipe rode for camp.

Four days went by. The men were growing

restless and there were endless rumors among them that the attack would begin any hour now. Clint and Felipe answered no questions from them on the subject and listened endlessly to the reports of the men who were sent off to keep watch on the area from various vantage points.

'Perhaps we have misjudged Mr. Lang,' Felipe said. 'Perhaps we must begin again.'

'Let's give it one more day,' Clint said.

They didn't need another day. That night, during the first watch, there was sudden cry of pain and some grunting, and then two of the men brought another Mexican between them to Clint.

'Where did you find him?' Clint asked in Spanish.

'We caught him snooping around the edges of the camp like a mongrel dog.'

'Who are you?' Clint demanded of the Mexican, whose face he couldn't make out very well by starlight.

'Señor, I am not an enemy. I am a messenger. I have a message for you from Señor Valenzuela.'

The mention of the hated name made the two men holding the messenger take firmer hold and shake him fiercely.

'Ah,' one of them said. 'From Valenzuela. I think, Señor Evans, it would be a fine thing to make of this man an example of what happens to pups of this filthy dog Valenzuela. I think we should disembowel him, and let his screams warn the other pups of Valenzuela what is in store for them.'

'Cool off, friend,' Clint said, realizing how close to the boiling point these men were. What would they do when they finally realized they were not to get a chance to torture all of Valenzuela's men to death?

To the messenger, Clint said, 'What is the message?'

The man took an envelope from his pocket and passed it silently to Clint.

Clint risked lighting a candle to read it by, aware he could be making a target of himself, if this was a trick of some kind. He saw the dimly lighted faces of the rows of the Mexican force, all watching with fierce interest, and the worried face of Valenzuela's man.

The letter was short. It demanded to know who the force of men belonged to, and what they were doing here. Clint used a quill to reply right on the same sheet of paper.

He wrote, in Spanish, that he was from Griego, and that since Felipe had come with the news that Pepita had been killed out of spite, Griego now wished to smite the filth Valenzuela and totally destroy him. He said that a way had been found to nullify the

188

defenses and that in a short while Valenzuela would lie begging at the feet of his captors. After a moment of mental debate, Clint added that there would be no mercy shown, and that Valenzuela would be treated with the same consideration with which he had treated Miguel and Pepita.

Clint folded the sheet of paper back up and sealed the envelope with drippings from the candle. Then he handed it back to the messenger.

'See Valenzuela gets this as soon as possible,' he directed.

'Sí, I will do this.'

But the two men would not let go of him. They were becoming angry.

'Why should we let this cowardly yellow dog go?' one man demanded. 'It is time to have an example, no?' He turned to the others, and got a rousing chorus of agreement.

'Let him go,' Clint instructed tersely.

'Señor Evans, this man is one who deserves to die, does he not? All the pups of the dog Valenzuela deserve to die, do they not? Why should we not begin when we may? It will strike the fear of God into the other pups of Valenzuela. The taste of the blood of this pup will be a good taste for we who starve for the blood of these filthy coward dogs!'

This brought another rousing chorus of

agreement. The messenger was growing pale, and he looked all around desperately at the fierce faces glowing readly brown in the candlelight.

'I think it would be a good thing for the men,' said Felipe, who had been awakened by all this. He sounded eager. 'It would satisfy their thirst, Cleent.'

The toothpick in Clint's mouth tipped up.

'Somebody has to take this message to Valenzuela. If this man is dead, one of you will have to go. Which of you will it be? You?' he said sharply, looking at the man who had been doing the talking. 'Or you?' he asked, looking at the other man holding the messenger.

For a moment Clint stared first one, then the other in the eye, unblinking, determined.

There was only the sound of the wind rustling in the trees overhead.

'Then let him go,' Clint said, and they did.

The man didn't waste time. He was gone inside of thirty seconds, and probably praying that he never had to act as messenger again.

There was a resentful jostling among Griego's men. Clint realized he might have won this battle, but in the end he could lose the war, and the men cut loose and start letting blood run freely in the dirt.

CHAPTER TWENTY-ONE

Just before dark two days later, the messenger came back again, looking terrified and wary. Everybody watched him hungrily. Clint thought if anybody looked like dogs it was Griego's men—starving dogs drooling over the sight of fresh meat.

Clint took the message and read it leaning against an oak tree.

It read, in Spanish: 'Querido Señor Evans, Señor Griego would have done better not to trust the scoundrel Felipe. He lies. I have not harmed Señorita Pepita in any way. I still wish to marry her, and she me. But I must have Señor Griego's blessing. Please return to Señor Griego my respect and inform him of this fact. Please tell him that I have never wished him evil and even now wish him no evil. I will not marry Señorita Pepita without the father's blessing, and she will not marry me, though she has promised me her hand as soon as Señor Griego's blessing is forthcoming. Quedo de usted su afmo. y S.S., Garcia Valenzuela.'

Clint looked at Felipe and nodded.

'What does he say, Cleent?' Felipe asked.

'What we wanted him to. Hand me the

quill.'

Clint wrote: 'I have my orders, Valenzuela. We will attack as planned. We do not believe you, quite frankly. However, if it is true, then you and she and one man alone should meet with myself and one man in the empty tool shack near the heading of the closed Jewel Mine. Your men and ours can watch from below that only the five of us enter the shack. It is too far to shoot accurately, so none of us will be in any danger. We will approach from the south, you from the north. Climb under the flume, if you wish cover until you get high enough. We will climb through the woods. I will give orders that my men are not to attack yours, and I suggest you do the same, or there will be a futile bloodbath. If Pepita is alive, Señor Griego has no desire for a bloodbath, but only to negotiate her release. This is what we will do in the tool shed. If you are not there by noon on next Sunday, we will assume you lie and we will attack. Do not underestimate our ability to destroy you, Señor Valenzuela. Señor Griego's men are thirsty for your blood.'

Clint sent the messenger off, and the men were silent, watching. The messenger disappeared along the winding trail under the trees. The camp began to be full of muttering and grumbling. One man finally came forward.

'Señor Evans,' he said, 'the men wish to know when we attack.'

'I will tell you when it is time for you to know,' Clint repeated the words he'd repeated many times before.

But this time, instead of the man wandering off disappointed, he remained standing in front of Clint belligerently.

'We demand to know, Señor,' he said bluntly. 'You have told us this so many times already that it wearies our ears to hear it. We demand to know now.'

'*I* don't know,' Clint said. 'How can I tell you? It depends on the outcome of these messages, and if the wind blows right. But if it is something to do you want, do not worry. Tomorrow there will be plenty to do.'

'We will make preparations?' the man said hopefully.

'Yes. There will be dynamite to load and wagons to drive.'

The man's eyes lit up at the prospect of dynamite. Clint was wondering if this part of the plan was so smart after all, given the eagerness of Griego's men. But he couldn't think of a better way to worry Valenzuela and keep the pressure on than to make a show of buying a lot of dynamite and wagons and burros and carrying it slowly and carefully towards the stronghold. It was bound to help make Valenzuela question even his impenetrable defenses. As long as it didn't also make Valenzuela think he ought to stay home and mind the store at any cost, things might work out all right.

The camp spent a restless night, as word spread quickly that the next day would see them handling dynamite. Clint imagined there would be a lot of dreaming about exploding Valenzuela pups.

In the morning, bright and early, they packed up and rode into town. Clint, using money supplied by Griego, bought five wagons and enough dynamite to fill them. It was an impressive lot of fireworks, and it wasn't long before the whole town was abuzz with the rumor that this small army was about to attack Valenzuela. Clint even heard of some money being placed on the event, and noticed men riding off towards the stronghold, perhaps some Valenzuela spies, or maybe Dixon men, and some probably hunting a good place to watch the excitement from.

It took all day to get the dynamite loaded into the wagons, and drive about halfway to the stronghold. They made camp in a spot above the trail, from which they could watch it in both directions. The spot was chosen also for cover and as being an easy place to defend, should Valenzuela decide to attack.

As he got into his roll that night Clint thought about all that dynamite. He wondered if he would be able to stall for the three days until Sunday without making his men impatient.

The next two days they spent moving the dynamite up over the crags short of the stronghold, straining and sweating and swearing at the burros, which now carried the load of fireworks. Clint's idea was to take it around the back side of the big rock where the woods grew thickly at its base, and the wall of rock overhung them, and set the men to work with star drills.

'Is not the wall very thick?' one of the men asked doubtfully.

'It is much thinner here than anywhere else,' Clint said, having no idea this was so. He'd picked this place for its cover and for the time it would take to get here and start work.

The third day saw the men working at the rock, sledging the star drills in an endless ringing din. Clint had men keeping watch in all directions, especially on the rim above, in case Valenzuela got too nervous and tried to attack. But the day passed uneventfully, and Clint was happy to see that the men were plum tuckered out by all the work they'd been doing, and he hoped this would temper their desire to attack Valenzuela's men the next day.

Clint spent a fairly sleepless night, thinking all the time he heard either Valenzuela's men coming or Griego's men going. But it was only night animals and the wind.

Sunday morning in the camp was full of talk about how long it might take to plant enough charges to blow a hole into Valenzuela's camp, or to reach China, whichever came first, and there were quite a few men who thought they'd come out in Shanghai first. Clint was tempted not to let the men in on what was to happen today at all, but let them just go on working while he and Felipe slipped quietly off to have their chance at Valenzuela. But if something went wrong, it would not be wise to have his backup force planting dynamite charges miles away from where they would be needed. And if Valenzuela had any wits at all, he'd be mighty careful in his checking to see just what he was walking into.

Clint told them to pack up, but hide the dynamite. They looked at each other at first in puzzlement, and then significantly. Clint did not inform them of anything but that they were going for a ride and not too long after, they rode.

It took, as Clint expected, until about eleven o'clock or thereabouts to get to the abandoned Jewel Mine, which was sunk in the rock face miles from any presently active mine. He had the men take up positions in a thicket and a large pile of slag. Then he sent out scouts to check the area under the old broken down flume that came down the rock face a quarter mile away. He warned them to be careful and watch their backs.

Half an hour later, they returned excited with the news that there was a whole pack of Valenzuela's dogs under cover in some rocks over there.

'Well, Felipe,' Clint said, 'this is it. Let's go.' To the men he said, 'I want you to watch that shack way up there by the shaft heading. We are going to try to rescue Pepita, so that she will not be in danger if we attack. Felipe and I are going in from one side, and Valenzuela and one man to side him and the girl from the other. If anybody else shows his nose, or starts up under the flume, attack those men over in the rocks. You can't hit the shack from this far away, but you can hit the men in the rocks and keep anybody else from going up. His men should have orders to remain below, and you are not to follow us. We will be back when we are finished. It may be some time.'

The men were puzzled, but willing, and Clint didn't tell them any more. He hoped they wouldn't think he was selling out, and on their own attack Valenzuela's force, if this took a while.

The climb was long and hot. Clint found his wounds paining him, even though they were mostly all just scars by now.

'Do you have your weapons, Cleent?' Felipe asked when they were part way up.

'I didn't check on that more'n a dozen times before we started.'

'What do you think Valenzuela will have?'

'Two or three guns and knives. He won't come unprepared. He may not come at all. This is a big risk for him. I'm surprised he's here.'

'He wants the mine, señor.'

'I guess Pepita must have refused him if he didn't get her father's blessing, or else Valenzuela doesn't know that Griego will feel obliged to keep his word to give her the mine whoever she marries.'

'Thees plans is working, Señor Cleent. We are going to get the cowardly dog, and it will be a great pleasure to cut out his eyes and his tongue and pull his fingernails one by one. I have thee pliers for this, Cleent, and I have a small saw to cut of his fingers one by one.'

Clint felt soured enough about Felipe's plans without hearing the fat Mexican talk about it. 'Save it, Felipe,' he said.

'But I take great pleasure in the anticipation,' Felipe said, as they kept on climbing through the scrawny growth of fir. 'It is something I have been waiting for for a long time, señor. I wish to savor it, you know?'

'Then do it quietly.'

'Sí, Cleent, if you wish. But you feel the same desire for the blood of Dixon that I have for the blood of Valenzuela. There is much pleasure in revenge, is there not? It is a fine thing, like much tequila or a pretty señorita with dark eyes and much desire.'

Clint was silent. Doggoned if he didn't hate Mexicans.

They arrived at a point even with the shack and the mine heading. A quarter mile away, he could see three small figures slowly moving up the rock face under the wooden flume. It was too far to be sure if one was a woman or not.

'Now listen, Felipe,' Clint said. 'We're going to be polite and not hurt anybody right away. We'll disarm them, and then talk. It may be Valenzuela will crumple when he sees we have the upper hand.'

'But it will be pleasant to torture Valenzuela to make him talk,' Felipe said eagerly. 'However, it will not matter to me, for sooner or later I will torture him until he dies screaming.'

'You're a bastard, Felipe, you know that?'

'But then you are too, are you not?'

'Shut your mouth.'

'It is the way the world passes, señor, no? Yours is not the only revenge.'

'I told you to shut your mouth,' Clint said curtly, and led the way out of the trees onto the heat of the bare rock.

The sun was as bad here as on the desert. The reflected glare of light and heat made his eyes water. They didn't even have the distance from the reflecting surface that riding a horse gave you in the desert.

The others a quarter mile away were also moving cautiously along the side of the steep slope of rock, picking their way along from crevice to ledge. As each side drew nearer the mine shaft headframe, the progress grew slower since everybody was busy holding a pistol in his hand, in case the other side should try something. Valenzuela had the further hampering of Pepita to cover. Clint could see the determinedly superior look on her face as she picked her way along.

Clint glanced down, and could see the two small armies sitting and squatting behind bits of cover, mostly looking up at the figures on the rock face.

When they reached the shack, Clint and

Felipe waited outside in full view for the others to come up.

'Hola, señores,' Valenzuela said, as though he were in his own stronghold welcoming friends. He was dressed immaculately, and Clint was amazed that the man had climbed all the way up here without getting dirt or dust on his clothes, and had only the slightest dew of sweat on his brow. His companion, an inscrutable Mexican in the Indian dress of his country, was sweating heavily. Pepita, wearing a dress and jewelry, was even more of a source of amazement. She looked cool and in command and as dignified as a queen. Clint mopped sweat from his brow with his shirt sleeve and looked at Valenzuela.

'Pepita, as you see, is very much alive and well,' Valenzuela said, watching them carefully. 'It surprises me that you bring along as your man the filth who lied to you about her death.'

'It's hot out here,' Clint said. 'Let's go inside.'

There was a little maneuvering to get inside without anybody becoming vulnerable. Then they all sat around on empty dynamite crates, with another box in the middle to serve as a table, though it was quite small.

'Pepita,' Clint asked, 'do you wish to marry this man?'

'No,' she spat out, as though it was coffee unexpectedly loaded with salt instead of sugar.

Clint looked at Valenzuela, who was shaken not one bit.

'Seems like the lady doesn't agree with your version of the story.'

Valenzuela smiled. 'Señor Evans, I know of you. You are a man who knows the way of the world, are you not? You are aware of what this is all about, are you not?'

'A gold mine. But I can tell you Valenzuela, you will never get it from Griego.'

'He will believe you, will he not?'

'I think so.'

'You might tell him that Pepita wishes to marry me, and he would agree to give his blessing, would he not?'

'It is possible. But people from Griego's family, and probably the old man himself, would wish to be at the wedding, and if Pepita does not wish the marriage, then she would be not long in letting this be known.'

'You must allow me to concern myself with that problem, señor. It is not impossible to overcome. But we are here to negotiate, are we not? It is a question of what might convince you to tell Señor Griego of Pepita's true wish to marry me.'

'Ah,' said Clint. He noticed Felipe's fingers

202

were itchy and hoped he wouldn't try something foolish before the agreed upon maneuver.

'You are not I am sure concerned with such elusive apparitions as the emotions of a woman,' Valenzuela said. 'You are similar to myself. You deal in real terms. You perhaps have a desire for wealth?'

'Please continue.'

'I am not a poor man, señor. I could make you very rich.'

'There is one thing I want,' Clint said. 'Dixon.'

'Perhaps one thousand dollars would recompense you for your efforts with Señor Griego?' Valenzuela said as though he had not heard Clint.

'Dixon.'

'It is possible I could go as high as two thousand.'

'Dixon.'

'It is not wise to push me too far, Señor Evans. Do not imagine that I fear a few paltry loads of dynamite and a motley assortment of Griego's vaqueros. But I will go the three thousand. That is my final offer.'

'It isn't wise to push me too far either, Valenzuela. But,' Clint added, grinning, 'four thousand would be just about right.'

'This would have to buy your silence

forever. I have many ears, and much determination and many guns.'

'I can't see why you care about that once you get your hands on the mine, but I don't talk much.'

'It is best not to upset Señor Griego.'

'Pepita will talk in any case.'

Valenzuela smiled thinly, looking at Pepita, who had sat completely aloof through this conversation, not even blinking. 'It is astonishing how many women die giving birth.'

Clint felt a knot forming in his stomach on account of this conversation. But it was over now. He stood up, held out his hand to Valenzuela.

Valenzuela stood up and looked a moment at the hand as though hesitant about taking it, and then smiled in a self-satisfied kind of way and reached for it.

Clint, smiling, yanked Valenzuela suddenly off his feet, tripping him over the box. At the same moment, Felipe slid his knife into Manuel's belly and twisted it. The man opened his mouth to scream and Felipe slit his throat. The man slumped with a gargling sound. Pepita had leaped to her feet and backed off towards the door. Now she was about to go out.

Clint meanwhile had rolled Valenzuela onto

his back on the floor and pinned him. Catching sight of Pepita at the door he said sharply, 'Stay in here, or you'll get us all killed.'

She hesitated and Felipe had a moment to pull her away and sit her down. Then, as Valenzuela twisted unexpectedly and started to get away, Felipe bounded over and squatted to get his pistol against Valenzuela's temple.

'It is time,' Felipe said, 'for you to stay quiet, my filthy cowardly friend.'

CHAPTER TWENTY-TWO

Clint got off Valenzuela and went to Pepita.

'It'll be all right now,' he said comfortingly. 'Soon you will be with your father again. But right now we must wait for darkness in order to escape. Otherwise a war will begin and it will be very dangerous to try to get away.'

'I understand,' Pepita said, calmly and collectedly. 'What are you going to do with this filth here?'

'Señor Valenzuela is going to get much practice screaming,' Felipe said, showing his yellow teeth.

'It is nothing more than he deserves,' Pepita

spat out.

'Señor Valenzuela,' Clint said, taking a seat near where Felipe had the bandit covered on the floor. 'It is not my wish to hurt you. As you know, I am interested in one thing only. The location of Dixon's place of hiding. If you will tell me that, I desire nothing else from you.'

Valenzuela was sweating now. For the first time he looked as though he had climbed the hot face of the rock.

'Please, señor,' he said. 'I will tell you.'

'See?' Pepita said. 'The man is a coward. He has no honor at all.'

Felipe had his knife out now, and holding it at Valenzuela's throat, which glistened with sweat, he said, 'I think I will begin with your eyes. I will cut them out like pits out of two fat plums, eh?'

'Back off, Felipe,' Clint said sharply. 'The man says he'll talk. Go ahead, Valenzuela. Tell me where I can find Dixon.'

'You will promise to let me go?'

Clint paused looking at Felipe. The fat Mexican's eyes were burning.

'What you did to Felipe's family is inexcusable. As you see, Felipe wants to make you die slowly and painfully. If you talk, I will see that you die quickly with a bullet through your head.'

Felipe looked at Clint, and Clint looked back. They said nothing. Clint could not tell what Felipe thought about this statement. Clint was not sure himself whether he meant what he said.

'I must be allowed to live,' Valenzuela said. 'I do not wish to die.'

'I'm afraid your time has come,' Clint said. 'It is only a matter of dying slowly and painfully or quickly and with little pain.'

Valenzuela squeezed his eyes tightly together and either sweat or tear water ran from the corners.

'I beg you,' Valenzuela said. 'Have compassion.'

'I have,' Clint said. This business sure did taste sour. He was sweating plenty, it kept running into his eyes, and he was wishing he hadn't come. Damn but didn't he hate Mexicans. He ought to let them all torture each other to death, if that was what they wanted.

Felipe moved his knife slowly towards Valenzuela's frightened eyes, which stared fixedly at the point of the knife.

'I will tell you,' he said shakily. 'But take this torturing killer away from me.'

'Back off, Felipe,' Clint said, and Felipe did so only with great reluctance. He kept Valenzuela covered with his pistol.

'Señor Dixon has a hidden stronghold in the mountains west of here. I will draw you a map. But I beg you, do not shoot me.'

'Ha!' Pepita said with disgust. 'Here is a man who is big enough to kidnap helpless women, but he cannot even die with dignity.' She spat on him, and Clint could see Valenzuela's neck turn a deep shade of red and his brows lower. Pepita had probably hurt him more with that statement than could anything even Felipe might do to him.

Clint had brought the quill pen and some ink, and they used the back of one of Valenzuela's letters. Valenzuela sketched for a while, and Clint looked it over carefully.

'It is about a three day journey,' Valenzuela said. 'But Dixon is not there at all times. He travels much, and has very many men to watch out for him. You will not be able to harm him, Señor Evans.'

Clint pocketed the paper. 'We'll see,' he said.

Felipe moved closer to Valenzuela, grinning. 'Now we cut off some pieces and see if he is telling the truth, eh?'

Clint said nothing. He had to make up his mind and jump one way or the other.

Felipe, still holding the pistol in one hand, brought out the saw with the other. It was a small cabinet-maker's saw with fine teeth.

'Señor!' Valenzuela said desperately. 'Please, señor, you gave your word!' He was begging Clint.

'You cannot hold the gun and use the saw both at the same time,' Pepita said to Felipe. 'Let me hold it.' Felipe paused a moment and then gave the pistol to her. She held it out in both hands, sighting it on Valenzuela's chest.

'Oh, señor,' Valenzuela moaned. 'I have told you the truth. If I am to die, what difference will it make to me what becomes of Dixon?'

'Felipe,' Clint said, 'I believe him. I have promised you revenge for the death of your family. You can either shoot Valenzuela clean and quick or fight him a fair fight, armed with knives or fists, or boxes or whatever you choose that will not make noise and set off a battle below.'

'I will have my revenge in my own way,' Felipe said quietly. 'I have told you many times how I will do it. Just as you will have your revenge in your own way upon Dixon.'

'I'm telling you what your choices are.'

'It will happen as I wish, señor,' Felipe said menacingly, and the knife flashed in the sun coming through the musty window as it turned to point at Clint.

'If I have to kill you, you won't get any revenge at all,' Clint said. His hand strayed near the hilt of his own knife.

'Keep him covered,' Felipe directed Pepita, indicating Clint, 'so that I may remove small pieces of Valenzuela without disturbance.'

'You're going to let a woman protect your ass for you,' Clint said.

Felipe leaped at Clint flailing the knife.

Valenzuela at that moment made a dash for the door. Clint was just becoming aware of that as he dodged Felipe, when Pepita set off Felipe's pistol, which was deafening inside the small tool shed. Valenzuela cried out and lurched to the side, bounced against the doorpost shaking the littly rattly wooden structure, and then crashed solidly through the door and was running away outside.

Pepita fired again and again and again, but didn't seem to hit anything. Felipe took the gun away from her and went out the door after him. Clint, gun in hand, followed.

Below, a shout went up and then shooting started hotly. Clint spared a quick glance down, saw smoke drifting off into the woods, and then quit thinking about that battle for the moment. There was the question of what to do now about Felipe and Valenzuela. Common sense told him that it was the time for him to get out. Valenzuela was running faster than Felipe was, being more agile. But Felipe had a gun and Valenzuela didn't. That

210

sort of evened up the odds. Clint figured he had what he wanted, and it was time to clear out. From here on, none of this was his business.

He stopped running north along the wall of rock after them and turned to look back at the shack. Pepita was standing outside it watching him.

He returned to her.

'Time for me to take you home,' he said. 'We'll have to be mighty careful how we move, but with some luck we can clear this passel of Mexican hotheads and get clean away.'

She looked at him blankly, and he realized he'd been talking English again, and that she didn't understand what he was saying. He repeated the essence in polite Spanish, and she looked as though she wanted to refuse for a moment, and then she nodded.

'My father will be very worried,' she said gravely.

'Then come on,' Clint said, and took her by the hand and started along south across the rock face.

He kept glancing down to see if the smoke had cleared enough for the men below to see what was happening up here, but they were at it hot and heavy, shouting and screaming and shooting. A lot of steam was being let off.

Clint decided he wanted nothing more than to get as far from it all as he could as soon as he could.

They reached the scrub growth and Clint helped Pepita down the steep and tricky slope. Gunsmoke drifted up from the fight and lazied through the trees like mist rising from a mountain pond in the early morning. The further they went, the worse it got, and the louder grew the sound of shooting.

Pepita's eyes were watering from the sting of the smoke. Clint led her rapidly through the brush to the place some distance from the shooting where the horses had been left. Several men were supposed to be guarding the animals, but evidently the lure of the fight had been too strong, and they had abandoned their posts.

Clint got Pepita up onto one of the best of the Mexicans' horses, and she hitched up her skirt and rode astraddle like a man, since the saddle wasn't made for side usage and there wasn't time to fool around being dainty anyway. Clint swung onto his own horse, and then sought out a couple of burros loaded with victuals and other travelling supplies.

As they moved quickly away through the trees towards the trail, smoke and noise surrounding them and filling their eyes and nose and ears, over the din of shooting there came the deep rumble and boom of a huge explosion.

Pepita started around.

'Some dynamite,' Clint told her. 'Guess they decided that as long as there were going to be festivities they might as well go whole hog.'

CHAPTER TWENTY-THREE

They had been riding for a couple of hours when Clint happened to glance over at Pepita and was startled to see tears pouring freely down her cheeks. This time it was not gunsmoke, since they'd left it far behind.

'What's wrong?' he asked her, in Spanish.

She looked at him quickly, and then away. She suddenly looked very young and very vulnerable. She was no longer the regal, fearless, proud Señorita Pepita Griego who had an uncompromising disdain for those who had captured her. She was just another girl who'd been terrified half to death and who was so relieved she was safe she was crying.

Clint didn't say anything more, and she didn't say anything either.

They rode into town about nightfall, but Clint decided it might be safer to find some

213

place out of the way to spend the night, in case any of Valenzuela's men were still around.

He found a little hidden hollow back of town with a spring and only two ways in or out. Clint cooked some beans, leaving out the spices, and got a shot at a rabbit, and they feasted. Apparently Pepita's taste wasn't so far gone she couldn't appreciate regular food, at least when she had starved herself for a while. He wondered if it was possible that she'd gone without food ever since being kidnapped. It seemed too long for anyone to possibly live without food. But she surely was hungry. She ate everything he didn't, and didn't seem full. He asked her if she wanted some more, and she said yes, with great dignity.

He wondered if feeding her too much all at once would be good for her. But she showed no illness yet, had kept down everything. He cooked up some more beans and a tortilla or two for her, and asked how long it had been since she'd eaten.

'I have eaten nothing for a week. Before that, I ate some of the time, but not all of the time. I wished to show Valenzuela that it was within my power to starve myself if I wished.'

'You really wanted to see him tortured?'

She looked at him with large steady dark eyes.

'He is an evil man. He deserves it.'

214

'Seems to me torture only makes a man just as low as the man he's torturing.'

She lowered her eyes to look into the fire, and they were deep and unfathomable. 'The church says one should turn the other cheek,' she said. 'But I do not see the good of this. It only allows the evil man to do more evil.'

'I'm for putting men like Valenzuela out of action,' Clint said. 'But I don't see any reason to torture them.'

'You do not wish to torture Dixon? You have said yourself that he has done horrible things to your wife.'

This was just what stuck in his craw about this business. He looked at Felipe and saw what a monster revenge had made out of him, and he saw that he himself had been just as bad for having been so bloodthirsty for Dixon all these years. It was true that he had daydreamed many times about making Dixon hurt plenty before he died. But watching Felipe had set Clint to doing some thinking.

'If Felipe had been about to tear Dixon apart little piece by little piece, would you not have wished him to do so? Or wished to take the knife from him and do it yourself?'

Clint looked at Pepita. She was gazing at him unblinkingly.

He looked into the fire.

'Probably,' he said. 'But I'm glad it wasn't

Dixon.'

'Señor, revenge is a pleasure. You agree that evil doers should be destroyed. Why should not those who have been wronged enjoy the destruction?'

'All right. Suppose you do. What about the fellow's friends and relatives? They will feel then as you have, and will come after you and enjoy torturing you. And then one of your relatives will become outraged and do the same thing, and it goes on and on. Everybody outraged at the lowdown honorless way the other side is acting, but saying treating them the same way is nothing more than they deserve. Think of all the pain and suffering that is caused this way. It might not end until both sides are wiped out, and everybody winds up writhing under the knife one time or another. Revenge is a bad thing, far as I can see. It isn't justice, it's just anger and feeling you're always right and the other fellow is wrong. It's all in how you go at it. If I'm going to kill Dixon, I shouldn't do it for pleasure or because I'm angry, but just to stop him from doing any more terrible crimes. It's a sad thing to have to kill a man.'

She shook her head in perplexity.

'I do not understand you norteamericanos. You deny your own joys when it is your right, and take your joy in ways that it is not right and hide it. It is a big difference.'

'I guess there's some truth in that. But it's not the point.'

*   *   *

The next day they rode down the stream under the oaks and then turned into the desert. Clint was deep in thought about what he would do once he'd brought Pepita safely home. On the one hand he had no desire to have anything to do with Valenzuela or Felipe or Griego or Dixon or anything connected with this business. He was thoroughly soured on them all and on his own desire for revenge. On the other hand, in spite of himself he was seething like a boiling pot of lead at Dixon. The way Clint saw it, Dixon was the cause of all the trouble. If not for Dixon, Valenzuela wouldn't have gotten where he had, and if Valenzuela hadn't gotten rich and arrogant as a bandit, he probably wouldn't have had the nerve to try kidnapping Pepita. And if Dixon hadn't touched Margaret, Clint wouldn't have ever come to these parts and gotten mixed up with Mexicans at all, and he wouldn't have cared what they did to each other anyway. The idea of Dixon getting away with that irritated Clint no end.

'Señor Evans,' Pepita said, 'you do not look

happy. You appear disgusted.'

'I am disgusted,' Clint said, and startled his horse into a short bound ahead by digging in his spurs unconsciously. Clint got more disgusted, because there was no good reason to treat his horse that way.

A week and a half later, not too much the worse for their long trip across the desert— still no Indians—they pulled up in the yard of the Griego hacienda. Crossing the ranges they had collected an excited bunch of vaqueros. A few had ridden on ahead to bring the news that Pepita was safe and so that a welcome could be prepared for her. She had for the first time Clint had seen begun to smile. It was quite a smile, and almost enough to make him glad he'd gone through everything.

The old man's bed had been carried outside and an awning set up over it. He was sitting up, and his eyes were moist as he watched them come up to him through the beds of flowers.

'Hola,' Clint said, feeling awkward. 'Brought your daughter back.'

'Pepita. . .'

'Papá. . .'

Clint watched them hugging each other and crying on each other's shoulders and felt even more uncomfortable. But he was glad for them.

218

'Señor Evans!' Griego's voice, much stronger now, rang out. 'You have succeeded! You have made me the happiest man who exists! You have given rest to my soul. Please, come here, señor, let me begin to thank you by shaking your hand.' Clint shook. 'Now, señor, we must celebrate, and then we must discuss what will give you happiness, eh?' The old man's eyes shone. Clint had a strong notion that it wouldn't be long now before Griego got out of bed.

To do what? Would he now send more men out after Valenzuela and torture him to death the way Felipe wanted to? Or was Griego different? Would he be satisfied to merely shoot Valenzuela? Or what?

Clint was sure Valenzuela deserved to die, but the thought of how Griego might be apt to do it tasted sour. The next thing would be some friend or relative of Valenzuela would go after Griego, and so on and so on as he had explained it to Pepita. But then, *he* hadn't any right to get high and mighty, not with the anger he felt at Dixon, and the overpowering desire that came over him off and on to see Dixon squirm for his crimes.

Griego clapped his hands and a servant came up. Griego had him bring fruit and tequila and told him to bring on the musicians. Clint hung around drinking and

219

dancing and listening to the songs and joyous yelling of Griego's hands. Everything became a blur and he got to feeling that he didn't really have any problems after all. He had a chance to dance with Pepita and with some other pretty señoritas and to drink tequila and he was having a good time, and the world looked just fine and everything seemed where it ought to be, so what could be wrong?

He stayed around for three days, while the festivities went on, and was drunk most of the time. But then he woke up early in the morning of some day he couldn't place, and it felt like he had awakened under a rock slide, his head was being pounded so hard.

It took him four hours to recover enough to get out of bed, and another two to get up enough nerve to leave the room. Things were quiet around the place, everybody sleeping it off. Clint wished he could have slept longer and wondered vaguely why he hadn't.

He hunted up his horse and saddle with considerable effort and packed some supplies aboard a burro, and then, gingerly, got into the saddle and set off north, leaving the whole hacienda still sleeping, though it was nearly noon by now.

He had decided to leave the hacienda, but he had not decided what he would do next. He wanted to go take care of Dixon, but the whole business of killing and treachery had left him with such a confused mixture of fury and disgust at his own uncontrolled anger that he didn't trust himself to walk into a showdown. He was afraid he'd go nuts and cut Dixon up with his knife and make him hurt for what he'd done, and then regret it afterwards and have to live with it the rest of his life.

He decided he wouldn't do anything for a while, but just drift along. He knew where to look for Dixon now, if he wanted him. He patted his pocket with the sketch of how to get there, and then his mind drifted off onto other things.

What had happened to the war that had gone on? Who was left alive, and did anybody figure one side or the other had won? And had Felipe caught up with Valenzuela?

Clint was curious, and like a moth flying into a candle, he rode north for Oak Creek.

CHAPTER TWENTY-FOUR

He was aiming to hit Crooked Creek and then go on north from there across the Mescaleros' hunting desert, but he missed and fetched Dead Flats instead.

It was just at dusk when he sighted the broken bunch of buildings, and he decided he might as well spend the night there as out in the open. So he pushed on as darkness fell and rode in under the stars.

He wished he hadn't come. The place made him uneasy. It wasn't just him either. The horse and the burro both felt it, for they shied and were reluctant to move forward.

Clint was about to turn around and ride back out into the desert again, when there arose over the empty silent town a piercing scream. It was loud and like nothing he'd heard before.

Clint tugged rein, getting his jittery horse under control, and sat listening hard. He was not sure if the scream had really been human or if it had been some animal.

At first thin and icy as mountain air, then reaching up to a full pitch of piercing strength, the scream rose again, and stopped, spent.

It came from somewhere at the far end of town. Clint wrestled his shying horse around and set his spurs. The burro leaned back against the tug on the lead rope with determination, and Clint didn't waste time with it but just dropped the rope and urged his mount on down the street.

The screaming was coming all the time

now, and Clint suddenly recognized the voice—Valenzuela.

The hairs stood up on the back of Clint's neck. Sweat prickled him all over. He felt sick. He wanted to swing his horse around and let it run clear of town, as the animal wanted to do. But there was just no way he could do that.

He pulled up and dropped down when he saw the dim forms of horses tied to the hitchrail in front of a rickety saloon. Inside there was the glow of a lantern.

Clint moved along to the gaping hole in the wall in which batwings had once flapped. They were now lying smashed on the ground just outside. Clint peered in, just as another scream rose.

There were three men inside. Two of them were leaning over the third. The lantern sputtered at its poorly trimmed wick, sooting the glass. It sat on the floor just beyond the three and shone on the fierce faces of the two leaning over, on the blood pooled around the man on his back on the floor, who was arched up with his head tipped back, eyes squeezed shut as he screamed. One of the other two men pulled his bloody knife from somewhere Clint couldn't see and the man's scream dissipated into a moan.

The man being tortured was Valenzuela all

right. And the man with the knife was Blake Dixon.

Clint couldn't figure it, unless Valenzuela had tried to cheat Dixon, or unless Dixon decided to move on Valenzuela while his forces were thinned out by the war with Griego. Was that what that letter had been about?

Dixon said something softly to his companion, like a couple of doctors conferring on an operation, and then the helper took hold of Valenzuela's hands and held them firmly in place on the floor. Dixon bent over Valenzuela with his knife.

Clint stepped in.

'Dixon!' he bellowed, raging.

The knife whizzed and if Clint hadn't ducked it would have pinned his neck to the doorpost. The helper went for his gun, and Clint shot him dead.

Dixon now went for his gun, and Clint shot it out of his hand. Then, looking at the blood on Dixon's hands, thinking of Margaret thrashing her life out with those hands around her neck, Clint hesitated.

Dixon's right hand dove into his clothes and out came a derringer. Clint shot Dixon through the heart, killing him cleanly and instantly.

He stepped over to look at Valenzuela.

'Please, Señor Evans,' Valenzuela said weakly. 'Shoot me. I am dying, but it is very ... painful ... slow.' The words cost him a great deal of pain.

Clint hesitated, and then made his decision and blew away half of Valenzuela's head with a forty-five slug.

Then he walked away.

Outside, he retched, leaning against the doorpost.

A few minutes later, ears ringing, he climbed weakly aboard his horse and rode out of town. Through the ringing he could hear the lonely clop of his horse's hooves in the silent empty town. He could smell burnt powder and scorched flesh.

The Presence watched him as he rode the length of the street and located his burro and then drifted out of town.

Out on the open desert, he noticed a gentle wind against his face, cool and fresh. He could smell jasmine for a moment, he thought, then it was gone and he figured it had to be his imagination.

He bedded down and figured he would do the burying in the morning. He was asleep in five minutes.

★   ★   ★

He rode into Oak Creek with only one purpose in mind: to find a job, most likely guarding a gold shipment north to the rails. In any case, a job that would get him away from here. If he landed at a railhead, he'd buy a ticket to somewhere, anywhere. He didn't care to see another Mexican or another desert again. Or another Dixon.

The warm air from the desert was sweeping through town, blowing up into the mountains. It was hot in the street even in the shade. Clint rode down the street slowly, hoping the peace of the town was real and the war between Valenzuela's men and Griego's was over.

There was a rattling sound from a doorway to the left, and Clint saw a sombreroed Mexican shaking his tin begging cup full of change. Clint was about to ride on, when the man spoke.

'Please señor, a few pennies for a poor blind man.'

Clint started: it was Felipe. Clint swung to the rail and hauled rein. He stepped over to Felipe and sat next to him on the doorstep in the sun.

'Felipe?'

Startled, Felipe turned as though to look at him, but his eyes were wrapped with a dirty cloth bandage.

'Señor Cleent?' Felipe said.

'What happened to you?'

'Oh, Señor Cleent, I am so glad to see you!' Felipe said happily, apparently unaware of the irony of his words. He put down the tin cup and reached out with his hands. Clint took one and shook it. Felipe's mouth smiled with delight. 'It is a long time, señor,' he said. 'I did not think I should see you again. Did you bring Pepita home safely?'

'Sure.'

'That is good, Señor Cleent. I am glad to hear it.'

'What happened?' Clint asked again.

'These?' Felipe said, pointing to his bandaged eyes. 'It is Valenzuela. I have him tied up and am about to have my revenge upon him, you know? But he is the tricky one, and the next thing he has *me* tied up. He uses a branding iron on my eyes. It is very painful, señor.'

Clint didn't think Felipe sounded upset enough to be talking about real events, and he yanked the bandage back.

It was like getting hit in the gut with a sack of flour. He gingerly replaced the bandage.

'Sorry, Felipe,' he said. 'You've told me so many lies.'

'I understand, Señor Cleent,' Felipe said, not sounding either offended or in pain. 'It is some time now. It does not hurt so much anymore. But I cannot see. I am a useless person now, am I not?'

'Valenzuela got his, Felipe. I saw Dixon torturing him. I shot them both, along with a man siding Dixon.'

'That is good news, señor. Everything is finished then. The fight it went on for three days, and myself, and Valenzuela and Dixon and one of Dixon's men are all that is left from this. It was a very bloody battle.'

'Want something to eat, Felipe?'

'I have just had something, Señor Cleent. But I am grateful that you ask me. What do you do now?'

'I don't know.' Clint pictured Felipe spending the rest of his life begging on this front step. 'Don't you wish Valenzuela had killed you?'

Felipe hunched his shoulders. 'I am grateful to be alive, señor. It is the Señor Dixon who saves me by attacking Valenzuela, so that I have a chance to escape. Cleent, it is not so awful. It is the way the world passes, no?'

'Hell of a jornado,' Clint muttered.

'Señor?'

'That's what somebody called it when we started out on this business. A day's ride. Hell of a long hard day's ride, seems to me.'

'Sí, it is true. But it is over, Cleent.'

Clint was not sure, but it seemed to him a change had come over Felipe. Maybe it was for the better.

'Want to ride with me?' he asked, before he thought.

'Señor! Señor Cleent, you do not know how happy this makes me! I cannot see, but I still have my wits, no? And you have your gun, no? We will go far, señor, I assure you.'

Clint was already having misgivings. Maybe it wasn't such a smart idea after all. It had been pity for Felipe that had made him offer. Felipe had paid for his part in the thing, and Clint was still plenty aware how angry he'd been when he killed Dixon. Looking at Felipe, he realized how little difference there really was between them on the matter of revenge. But for all this, Felipe was still Felipe, and next thing you knew he'd be up to something.

*   *   *

Two riders lifted a rise of dust on the desert as the sun sunk flaming towards the horizon.

'One thing,' the tall lanky one in the sweaty stetson said.

'Sí?' replied the short fat sombreroed one.

'There won't be any more doing favors for relatives.'

229

'No, señor.'

'Or telling me one thing and then doing something else.'

'Of course not, señor.'

'And no more of this señoring business. The handle's Clint.'

'Sí, Cleent. You have told me this before. It is not necessary to repeat.'

'The name is *Clint*. It has an "i" in it.'

'I do not know what the good is of learning to spell, Cleent, since I cannot see, but I will try nevertheless to learn.'

'C-l-*i*-n-t. Clint.'

'C-l-*i*-n-t. Cleent.'

The tall man's jaw clamped shut and the toothpick between his lips pointed at the violent sky.

Photoset, printed and bound in Great Britain by REDWOOD BURN LIMITED, Trowbridge, Wiltshire